DARK PICASSO

Nicole Tang Noonan Mystery #3

By Rick Homan

WWW.RickHoman.com

First published 2019
Copyright 2019 by Rick Homan
www.RickHoman.com

This is a work of fiction. Names, characters, places and incidents are either a product of the author's imagination or are used fictitiously. Any resemblance to actual persons living or dead, establishments, events, or locales is purely incidental.

Acknowledgements

I am grateful to my Sisters in Crime (and brothers); my fellow writers and the librarians at the Mechanics' Institute Library in San Francisco; my designer, Zach McGinnis, and my editor, Adam Gallagher, and most of all to my wife, Ann.

Rick Homan

Chapter 1

Pat turned off the interstate, and I gave him directions for the series of turns on state and county roads that led to the Milmans' home. The dinner invitation did not give a street number. The address was simply "Fairhaven" on Route 378 near mile-marker 17.

We turned where a low brick wall ran along the road marking the entrance to a driveway and drove between a cornfield and a pasture. The cornfield seemed to go on forever; the pasture ended at a stand of mature trees a half mile away.

As we passed the trees, the driveway curved and the house was revealed, still perhaps a quarter mile away. It looked like an English country house, built of red brick, two stories high. I counted four French windows on either side of the entrance with a second-floor window above each. It was big, but its proportions were graceful. Mature trees were clustered at either end to frame it in its hillside setting. It was not something I expected to see in Ohio farm country.

"Do you think that house cost more than all the buildings on campus put together?" I asked.

"Maybe not all the buildings," said Pat, "but, at least two or three."

"What are we doing here?"

"Professors at a dinner party in a house like this can mean only one thing, development."

"Development of what?" I asked.

"Donors."

Rick Homan

He leaned over and kissed me. I took a moment to enjoy the beauty of his sparkling green eyes, sandy hair and pale complexion.

When we reached the stone pavement in front of the house, a young man wearing slacks and a sweater waved us to the left, indicating where to park. "Welcome to Fairhaven." he said. "This way, please." We got out of the car and followed him into the house.

He led us through the foyer and into a room large enough to accommodate two groupings of sofa and chairs. One group was upholstered in pale blue and the other in pale yellow. The far wall had three sets of French windows opening to the garden. The room was flooded with late-afternoon sunlight.

From a blue armchair, a woman rose and walked toward us with her right hand extended. "Hi! I'm Tiffany," she said.

She was a few inches taller than me, five-three or four, and probably in her mid-fifties. She had big blue eyes, a sweet smile, and her curly blonde hair bounced when she talked.

Her long skirt and matching jacket in a pale rose color were accented by a necklace of what I assumed were real stones—sapphires since they were blue. I was feeling a bit somber in my classic "little black dress" with a single pearl on a chain, but I was secure in knowing it could never be inappropriate.

Tiffany scanned my face, taking in my Asian eyes, prominent cheekbones, and freckles on the bridge of my nose and under my eyes. Almost everyone took a moment to study my face when they first met me. My Chinese-American mother and Irish-American father had combined to give me an unusual look.

"Nicole Tang Noonan," I said. "And this is my friend, Pat Gillespie."

Tiffany took his hand in both of hers and said, "Welcome. Are you with the college too?"

"Yes," said Pat, "I'm in the psychology department."

Tiffany smiled, and said, "Oops! I said, 'college.' I still

think of it as Fuchs College. I can't get used to saying 'Cardinal University.'"

"We're all still getting used to it," said Pat.

Last fall, when the new School of Business opened, Fuchs College became a university and changed its name to Cardinal because nobody wanted to wear a t-shirt that read "Fuchs U."

While they were speaking, I was looking at a pair of landscapes that hung on facing walls. Both showed trees around a pond with low-angled light leaving the scene in partial darkness.

"Oh, do you like my paintings?" asked Tiffany.

"They're lovely," I said.

"They're by a local artist. One is called *Sunrise* and the other is *Moonlight*. They're almost the first ones I bought when we were looking for some pictures to put in this big old place." She glanced over my shoulder and said, "This is my husband, Dale."

We turned and saw a tall thin man coming from the corridor on our right. His hair was buzz cut, and he wore thick black glasses, which did nothing to soften his bony face. His green golf shirt tucked into black slacks, worn with black penny loafers, gave a no-nonsense impression.

After Tiffany introduced us, he said, "Great! I've been looking forward to meeting Tiffany's art friends."

Tiffany shot him a look and said, "They're not 'art friends.' They're professors at Cardinal University."

He raised his eyebrows to indicate, "Wow," without saying it. "Are you both in art?"

"Nicole is a professor of art history," said Pat. "I'm in the psychology department."

"Uh-oh!" said Dale. "I'd better watch what I say."

"Don't bother," Pat replied. "I already figured you out."

Dale let out a belly laugh. "I like this guy!" He slapped Pat on the back.

Pat flinched and seemed to hold his breath for a moment. I knew this was because he's sensitive about being hit, especially when it's unexpected. I was glad he was able to control his impulse to hit back. He works out a lot and has big arms and shoulders.

"Let's sit down," said Tiffany, waving us toward the blue sofa and chairs, opposite the fireplace.

Two young women in servants' uniforms appeared. One brought a tray with glasses of sparkling wine, the other a tray with canapés on little plates.

"I'm glad to have a real art expert here," said Dale, turning to me. "I've been hoping someone can give me some figures for the risk-adjusted return on the different kinds of art Tiffany has been buying."

I almost choked on my ahi tuna. "I'm afraid I don't have that expertise. I'm a historian."

"Dale is in finance," said Tiffany. "If it's not about money, he's not interested."

"That's not true. I'm interested in lots of things, but sooner or later everything involves money. Am I right, Pat?"

Pat looked him in the eye and said, "That's right."

"Dale, let's not talk about investments. Art is my hobby," said Tiffany, turning to Pat and me. "I enjoy learning about it. I want to become a connoisseur."

I didn't know whether to compliment her on having high aspirations or ask her if she knew what that word really meant.

The young man who had met us in front of the house brought another couple in from the foyer.

"Here's Anne and John," said Tiffany, rising and walking over to greet them.

"A couple of our friends from the club," said Dale, as he followed her.

Returning to her seat, Tiffany said, "Nicole, Pat, these are our friends from the club, Anne and John Ghent."

Anne was dressed in a sleeveless orange shift, and she carried a white sweater over her arm. She wore her straight brown hair in a severe cut, walked like a runway model, and had the muscles of an athlete. John looked older, or at least more worn, and his tweed sport coat looked a size too big for him.

Before Tiffany could tell them our names, Anne sat in the chair nearest Pat. "Hello there, gorgeous," she said, sizing him up.

I estimated the distance from where I sat to the chair where Anne sat and wondered if I should aim for her throat with my plate of canapés or hit her right between the eyes.

Chapter 2

As the servants arrived to supply the Ghents with food and drink, Dale looked across at John and asked, "Did you check out that stock I told you about?"

John shook his head. "Too rich for my blood."

"It went up eighteen percent today."

John managed a shrug.

Tiffany leaned in and whispered loudly enough that everyone could hear, "I don't think our guests want to spend the evening talking about investments."

Footsteps from the corridor announced the arrival of more guests. Dale got up and gave Tiffany a palm-down signal, inviting her to stay with us while he went to greet them.

Tiffany turned to me and said, "Anne is also an art collector."

I looked across at Anne and asked, "Is there a particular period that you collect?"

She kept her heavy-lidded gaze on Tiffany for a few seconds before turning to me and saying, "Modern painters. I'm not particular. We don't have that much. Wait until you see Tiffany's collection."

"Oh, but Anne," said Tiffany, "you have some very nice pieces." Her words were mild, but her cheeks blushed, and she had to suppress a smile. Clearly she liked Anne's compliment.

Laughter from the corridor got our attention. Dale came into the room with his arm locked around the neck of a heavy-set man dressed in a yellow golf shirt and green slacks. "I keep telling this guy he has to correct that slice, but he won't listen,"

Dale announced.

"Alright, alright," said the shorter man, patting Dale's arm in an effort to break free.

Dale released him and said, "The score was even halfway through the back nine, and this guy slices his drive into the woods. Never did find it. We had a pretty good bet on that hole too."

Anne's head swiveled to her right so she could speak to Dale over her shoulder. "Haven't you figured it out yet, Dale? They all let you win so they can stay on your good side."

The room went silent at this remark. Even at a distance, I could see Dale's jaw muscles flexing.

Glancing toward the archway, I noticed a petite woman with wavy salt-and-pepper hair. Her eyes focused on a table full of knick-knacks in the corner. She seemed content to wait until someone noticed her.

"For heaven's sake, Dale," said Tiffany. "You might want to introduce our guests." Turning to me she said, "Ernst and Maria Becker."

Dale pointed at John and Anne as he spoke to the Beckers. "You already know these guys from the club, and these folks are from Cardinal University. They're . . . um . . . ."

"Nicole Tang Noonan," I said.

"Pat Gillespie," said Pat as he stood and offered his chair to Maria, who smiled and accepted it.

"Oooh, a gentleman!" said Anne.

Pat said nothing but side-stepped toward me and stood within arm's reach of my shoulder.

I forced myself to set my now-empty plate on the coffee table in front of me, but I swore to myself: one more remark about my boyfriend and this woman would die.

Pat and I listened politely to some chatter about business, the law firm, and activities at the country club. I was making an effort to look interested when Tiffany heard someone in the corridor, stood, and said, "Nicole, Pat, come with me. I want you to meet some people."

We followed her to the archway and met a man and woman in their thirties. "These are my friends from the Greenbrae Art Museum," said Tiffany. "Have you been there?"

"No," I replied. "I'm new to the area and still have a lot to discover."

"Curtis Diaz," said the man, offering to shake hands. "We opened to the public only about six months ago."

"Curtis is the director of the museum," said Tiffany.

His gray wool suit hung well on his slender frame, complemented by a white shirt, and yellow patterned tie.

Tiffany continued. "And Sandra is the . . . the what? . . . you're in charge of all the artwork."

"Registrar," said the woman. She had a tanned athletic look and short-cut blonde hair. She offered her hand and said, "Sandra Carlini."

Before I could ask about the Greenbrae Art Museum, one of the servants approached and told Tiffany, "Dinner is served."

"I got those from that dealer in Columbus," said Tiffany from her seat at the end of the table, as I looked over three bright, colorful paintings of outdoor produce markets on the walls of the dining room.

"The same dealer who sold you the landscapes in the reception room?" I asked.

"Yes. I thought . . . dining room . . . pictures of food . . . why not?"

"Very nice," I said.

The servants came and took away the bowls from the first course, which was a spicy chilled corn soup. While they were serving the main course of Cornish game hens, asparagus, and mashed potatoes, Ernst Becker, seated to my left, said, "I confess I don't know a lot about art, but I'm fascinated. Did I hear that you are an art professor?"

"Yes, art history."

He smiled and nodded. "Do you specialize in Chinese

art?"

I fortified myself with a sip of the white wine. This was not the first time someone had assumed that, because I look Asian, all my interests must be Asian. "No," I said. "I'm from California. My dissertation was on California Impressionism."

"Ah, California," he said. "I keep trying to get Maria to take a vacation out there. I spend too much time in my office at the law firm. I could use some sunshine."

"You can't be spending all that many hours in the office," said Anne Ghent, who was seated on the other side of Ernst.

Ernst hesitated before saying, "I'm not sure what you mean."

"I hear you're losing clients," she replied, "and that the firm's finances are a little shaky."

Ernst's table knife slipped from his fingers and rattled on the table top. "We're doing just fine," he said. He sounded as if his throat were dry.

Across the table from Anne Ghent, Maria Becker sat with her head leaned to one side and her shoulders slumped, but her eyes were like daggers aimed at the woman who had just insulted her husband.

Across from Ernst, John Ghent slouched in his chair and kept his eyes on the plate of food in front of him. Apparently, he had long ago learned to ignore his wife's cruelties.

"You don't need to worry about my buddy, Ernst," said Dale from the other end of the table. "He's got all the billable hours he can handle keeping me out of jail."

"Goodness, Dale," said Tiffany, raising her voice to be heard from the other end of the table, "since that's not true, you probably shouldn't joke about it."

Dale drank almost half a glass of wine in one swallow, and said, "Anne, you're such a tease. When are you going to run away with me?"

Anne shrugged and said, "I've been waiting for you to ask."

In the silence that followed, I concentrated on cutting the

flesh of my game hen from the bones, while trying to think of some topic of conversation that wasn't likely to blow up in our faces. I glanced at the head of the table and saw Tiffany eating her food with a look of detachment on her face, though her hand trembled.

Pat came to our rescue. "I hear there's been a building boom around Columbus."

That was all the company needed to start sharing stories of real-estate deals, new developments, highway improvements, and upgraded utilities. The gossip and speculation kept us from having to focus on ourselves through the rest of the meal, which included lemon meringue pie.

When the dishes were cleared and everyone had complimented the hosts on a delicious dinner, Tiffany rose and said, "Will the ladies follow me into the drawing room?"

Chapter 3

Tiffany opened a door in the corner of the dining room. Sandra and Maria rose and walked through.

Tiffany said, "Why don't you join us too, Curtis? I have a couple new pieces in my collection I'd like to show you."

Curtis got to the door at about the same time as Anne, who turned to him and said, "You're just one of the girls, Curtis."

It seemed to me his back stiffened as he waited for her to walk through the doorway before him.

As I entered the drawing room, I paused to look out the French windows at the garden, which was just beginning to bloom.

Maria Becker joined me and whispered, "I'm sorry you had to meet Anne this evening. I wish I could say she isn't always like this, but unfortunately she is."

I forced a smile and said, "Well, it's really none of my business."

Tiffany's voice rang out from across the room. "Would you ladies care for coffee?"

"Yes," I replied, glad for the excuse to avoid further gossip from Maria.

I stopped in the middle of the room to take in the collection of artwork on the walls around me. At a glance it was obvious the collection represented a substantial investment in modern paintings. I saw three landscapes in the style of the Barbizon school.

Elsewhere, the unmistakable style of Marc Chagall caught

my eye in a dreamy scene done in gouache involving a horse's head, a flying woman, and stars. A painting of boats in a harbor might have been by Seurat. A simple painting of a vase of flowers showed the influence of early Picasso, but was probably not by him.

It was surprising to see a pencil drawing among all these paintings, but the powerful depiction of a voluptuous nude woman was clearly the work of a master. I guessed it was by Matisse. It might easily have cost as much as any of the paintings.

Overall, I guessed there was at least a million dollars' worth of art in front of me, probably more.

One painting hung above the fireplace and might have been worth more than all the rest combined. It was a depiction by Picasso of a couple embracing, about five feet by four feet. Their bodies were twisted into impossible positions; their limbs wildly distorted to suggest movement and energy rather than literal shape. The clash of lines and shapes gave the work an overall sense of desperation that recalled Picasso's landmark work, *Guernica*, but which seemed strange in a picture of an erotic subject.

There was one detail I had never seen in a painting by Picasso. Among the twisted limbs was a penis reaching out from the man's body and parting the woman's labia. Picasso showed genitals on both male and female figures throughout his career, as do many artists, but I had never seen a painting in which he explicitly portrayed the sex act. Because of the almost violent tone of this painting, Picasso seemed to ridicule his subject.

"Nicole? Your coffee?"

"Yes, thank you," I said, and took a seat.

"This is by Theodore Rousseau," Tiffany said to Maria, apparently answering a question about one of the landscapes. "He painted *en plein air*. That means in the open air. He and some others did that to get closer to nature."

Maria nodded as if suitably impressed.

"I bought it at Greenbrae's auction," said Tiffany, smiling at Curtis.

"When was that?" asked Maria.

"January of last year," said Curtis. Turning to me, he explained, "We selected thirty-seven works for de-acquisition and sold them through Christie's."

"I'm glad you got it," Sandra said to Tiffany. "You kept it in the neighborhood, so to speak, and it's a nice one. It looks good in here."

"Have you ever seen a painting you didn't like?" Anne Ghent sounded like she was demanding an answer.

Sandra thought for a moment. "I'm sure I have."

"Tell us about it," said Anne.

"None comes to mind at the moment. Why do you ask?"

"I wonder," said Anne. "Do you really have opinions about these things or is it your job at Greenbrae to flatter the taste of people who make donations."

"I'm the registrar at Greenbrae," said Sandra. Her voice sounded just as steely as Anne's. "It's my job to maintain an accurate, detailed inventory of the museum's holdings."

I wasn't sure about anyone else, but I was ready to call this a draw. "Your Picasso is spectacular, Tiffany," I said, doing my best to signal a new topic of conversation.

She smiled at me. "Thank you. It's one of his later works. Toward the end of his life he went into seclusion and produced many works that build on his earlier styles."

No one else picked up the topic, and with Anne in the room I feared exposing the painting to further comment. So, I set my coffee cup on an end table, and said, "I must excuse myself. We have a long drive back to campus."

Once Pat and I were on the freeway heading south, I said, "I didn't know Tiffany was going to split us up after dinner. What did the guys talk about?"

"It was just more of the same, golf and business deals."

"That must have been boring for you."

"Not entirely. I played enough golf in my early years to hold up my end of the conversation."

"You never told me that."

"Where I come from, boys are expected to play some kind of sport. I noticed guys playing football, basketball, and baseball seemed to get injured a lot, so I took golf lessons. I quit when I went to college."

After passing a slow-moving truck, Pat asked, "What did the women talk about?"

"Tiffany's art collection. She has more than a dozen paintings. One of them is by Picasso. It must have cost her a bundle. It's odd, too. I've never seen anything like it. It looks like a Picasso, but it has elements that aren't typical of his work. I'd like to find out more about it."

"That must have been fun for you."

"Not entirely. The way she talked about these paintings, it was as if she had memorized her comments from a catalogue or textbook. Do you remember when we arrived, and she was talking about those two landscapes in the reception room?"

"Yeah. She was really enthused about them."

"Right. But she doesn't get excited about these expensive paintings. It's more as if she respects them."

"Maybe she was feeling worn down by then. It was a long evening and, in some ways, a difficult one."

"It didn't get any easier when we moved into the drawing room. Anne Ghent practically accused Sandra of flattering Tiffany in order to attract a donation for the art museum."

"You may have noticed she said things like that all evening. She told Dale he didn't really win at golf. She implied Ernst's law firm was going out of business. She called Curtis 'one of the girls.' She humiliated her husband and Tiffany by flirting with Dale when he flirted with her."

"She flirted with you too."

"Yes, and that had nothing to do with me. She said those things to make you squirm."

Recalling all the obnoxious things Anne had done during

the evening was making my skin crawl. "This is crazy. What kind of person goes to a dinner party and spends the evening thinking of ways to make people uncomfortable?"

"They're called sadists. They don't all inflict physical pain for sexual gratification. Some get pleasure from embarrassing people or provoking them to anger."

I reached over and squeezed the muscles on top of his shoulder. "How did I ever get through life without a psychologist to explain these things to me?"

He smiled. "I can't imagine."

I sat back and sighed. "I hope I did my duty for good old Cardinal University tonight. What do you think? Did I develop a donor?"

"Do you feel like you're on speaking terms with Tiffany?"

"Sure. In fact, I might give her a call to find out more about that Picasso."

"Okay, then," he said. "She has a relationship with the university. Mission accomplished."

"I hope so," I replied. "I didn't even mention the gallery on campus. With everything else going on, I forgot."

"I'm sorry it was such a stressful evening for you. If you're tired, I can drop you off at your place."

"No! It's our night."

After we'd been seeing each other for about three months and had gotten serious, Pat and I found it awkward to keep asking one another if and when we should spend the night together. So, we declared Saturday our night. It could be cancelled only under the most dire circumstances. Of course, we also left ourselves free to spend other nights together during the week, morning classes allowing.

"If you're sure you feel up to it . . ." said Pat.

"You just drive the car," I replied as I lowered the back of my seat. "I'm going to take a little nap so I'm rested and ready when we get to your place."

Rick Homan

Chapter 4

On Sunday afternoon following the dinner party from hell, knowing I wouldn't be able to concentrate on my regular academic chores until I understood the odd characteristics in Tiffany's Picasso, I walked over to the library, found a biography and catalogues from two major exhibitions in the 1980s and 90s, and downloaded a recent article about his late work.

A few hours' reading confirmed what Tiffany said about the great artist living in seclusion during his last years and continuing to invent new ways to communicate with visual images. By one estimate, he averaged more than ten paintings per month for most of a year. There is no way of knowing exactly how much he accomplished in these years because he gave away many of these paintings to private collectors and kept no records of the gifts. Judging by the work he donated to museums, his innovations during these last years were as important as those that made him famous early in his career, such as Cubism.

I also learned that critics and historians have struggled with the bizarre tone of many of these late paintings—the sense of desperation, the air of ridicule, the sexually explicit images—just as I had when I looked at Tiffany's Picasso. Initially these works were dismissed as the scribblings of a great mind that had become demented, but eventually the money to be made by selling them overcame these criticisms and they began to appear in galleries.

Far from satisfying my curiosity about Tiffany's Picasso, this information set my mind spinning. I had to see that painting again.

I sent Tiffany an email thanking her on behalf of Pat and myself for the wonderful evening and saying that seeing her painting had prompted me to read up on Picasso's last years. I suggested we meet some time to talk about it.

While I was at it, I wrote to Sandra Carlini, asking if Thursday afternoon would be a good time for me to visit the Greenbrae Art Museum.

Within half an hour Tiffany wrote back, saying she was eager to know what I had learned about Picasso's late work and asking if I could come for tea Tuesday afternoon at three. I was glad to accept, hoping I could satisfy my curiosity. If, while I was at it, I helped my university develop a donor, so much the better.

The approach to Fairhaven was no less astonishing the second time. When I got to the door, a woman in her fifties, dressed as if she worked in a corporate office, introduced herself as Tiffany's secretary, and showed me into the drawing room. She said Mrs. Milman would be with me in a moment and left.

I stood back to study the Picasso. It was, as I remembered it, a study of two bodies caught up in a frenzy of motions, full of cartoonish exaggerations, but somehow it lacked energy.

A great work by a master is more than the sum of its parts. A work by a student may look very similar, but will feel like he labors to achieve his effects. A masterpiece seems effortless. This painting did not have that star quality.

Of course, not every painting from the hand of a master is a masterpiece. Picasso painted his share of failures, more so probably in his last years when he turned out so many paintings.

Tiffany came in from the corridor with a big smile on her face. "Tea will be here in a moment."

As we sat, I thanked her for inviting me back.

"I was happy to get your email," she replied. "I have so much to learn about art. I bought an art history book, but I haven't read very much of it."

"Which one?" I asked. "Do you remember the author's name?"

"Something like 'Jensen.'"

"Janson?"

"I think so."

"Great book, but it's practically an encyclopedia."

"Yeah, it's really big. I looked up the names of these painters in the index," she said, waving at her collection, "and then read about them, but there was so much in there I got lost."

"That can happen. Since you're interested in modern painters," I said, scanning the dozen-and-a-half works on the wall, "you might do better with some books on specific styles and maybe some biographies. Exhibition catalogues are good too because their essays aren't too long and they provide context."

"Okay. I'll have to get some of those."

"If you like, I'll write down a few titles and email them to you."

"Would you? That would be such a big help."

"Sure," I said. It was nice to see her smile again.

A maid brought in the tea tray, set it on the table in front of us, and left. Tiffany poured the tea.

"Cream and sugar, please," I said in response to her gesture.

I took a macaroon from the serving plate and bit into it. Bliss! I had to find out where she got these. Or perhaps I shouldn't know.

Tiffany set down her tea cup, and asked, "So what have you found out about Picasso?"

"Oh, I just read a few things Sunday afternoon. I hadn't realized how controversial the late paintings are."

"Are they really?"

"Yes, they are, partly because he painted so many, gave a lot of them away, and didn't keep records. What is the provenance of this one?"

"The province? You mean like where he painted it?"

"No. The provenance is the history of this particular painting, a list of all the people who have owned it and all the times it's been sold. Ideally it traces ownership all the way back to the artist."

Tiffany looked worried. "I bought it from the Redburn Gallery in New York. They didn't give me a list."

"That's alright," I said. "This painting is less than fifty years old. It may have had only one owner. It would be nice to think you bought it from the person who got it from Picasso."

"I guess so. Still, I think I should check. I'm going to call them."

The conversation wasn't going the way I'd hoped. I hadn't wished to cast doubt on her purchases.

"So, are Picasso's late paintings controversial for other reasons?" asked Tiffany.

I glanced at the painting and said, "Many of them are more sexually explicit than the earlier work."

Her eyes widened. She looked at the painting, then looked back at me. "I'm not sure what you mean."

"If you look just below center and to the right . . ." I said.

Tiffany looked for a few seconds and then gasped. She stood and walked across the room to stare at the painting. When she turned back to me she was scowling. "They're actually doing it."

"I didn't notice right away when I looked at it Saturday evening," I said. "There's so much going in in this picture, I don't think it's obvious."

I wasn't sure Tiffany heard what I was saying because she had turned away and was staring through the French windows out to the garden.

I waited for perhaps a minute, wanting to break the silence, but afraid to say anything else.

When she turned back to me, her face was expressionless. "Would you excuse me, please?" She left the room.

I helped myself to a partial refill on the tea. While I sipped it, I reviewed our conversation, trying to understand where I had gone wrong, but I didn't see how I could have played it any differently.

The secretary who had answered the front door came in and said, "Mrs. Milman isn't feeling well and won't be able to rejoin you. Can I get you anything else?"

"No, thank you," I said, putting my tea cup down. "I should be on my way back to campus."

As I drove, I wondered why Tiffany was so upset. Had I been in her situation, I might have decided to move the painting to a bedroom or some other private place, or I might have sold it, but I don't think I'd have been so embarrassed that I had to run and hide. Of course, I may have upset her by raising the question of provenance, though I'd tried to explain that shouldn't be a problem.

When I got home, I sent Tiffany that list of books about modern painters, thanked her for the tea and the opportunity to look over her collection, and offered to help her learn more about her paintings. I hoped I hadn't done any damage that couldn't be undone.

On Wednesday evening, I had dinner at Pat's house. As we ate, I filled him in on my visit with Tiffany the day before. "Obviously she was upset about having such a sexually explicit image hanging on the wall of her drawing room."

"She really hadn't noticed?"

"No. I'm sure she hadn't. She just stood there, staring out at the garden, as if she was trying to figure out where she had gone wrong."

"What do you think she'll do?" he asked.

"Probably go to the dealer and get her money back."

Pat smiled. It was a nice smile. "That's not the only shocking story to come out of our Saturday-night dinner party," he said. "Have you been following the local news?"

I shook my head.

"You remember Anne Ghent?"

"Yes."

"She's dead."

"Dead? How? What happened?"

"I'm not sure. I had the TV on in the living room when I was getting ready for bed last night, and I heard her name mentioned. By the time I came out of the bedroom and looked at the screen, they were showing footage of a crime scene in the parking lot of one of those big shopping malls south of Columbus. They said she had been shot and there were no suspects."

"Shot? Oh my God! Do you suppose someone jumped her in the parking lot and robbed her?"

"I don't know. I checked online this morning and the police aren't saying."

"This was just last night?"

He nodded.

"Wow. That is really scary. You just never know when something like that is going to happen."

Pat stared out the dining room window and suppressed a smile.

"What?" I asked.

"Nothing," he said, trying harder not to smile.

"Oh, come on! What are you thinking?"

He finished chewing a bite of his burger and swallowed. "You said, 'you just never know,' but I was thinking that with some people it's almost predictable."

I had no idea where he was going with this. "What are you talking about?"

"When we were driving home Saturday night, we talked

about all the ways she had tried to ruin the evening for everyone present."

"Yes, I remember."

"So, I was just thinking it's not hard to imagine someone wanting to get rid of her."

"Pat! That's a terrible thing to say."

"You're right. Is a country-club lawyer like Ernst going to blow someone away just for suggesting his business was failing?"

"Of course not," I said, but then I was the one trying not to smile. "But I bet his mousey little wife would."

"Oooh, listen to you."

We got, up stacked the plates, and took everything out to the kitchen to wash.

"What about the folks from the art museum, Sandra and Curtis?" asked Pat.

"Nah, they may not have liked her, but she was a potential donor."

"How can you be so cynical?"

"I work in the arts. Who do you think could have done it?"

Pat gave my question serious consideration before saying, "Maybe Tiffany's husband, Dale. Anne put a few dents in his ego, and he struck me as a bit of a narcissist. They generally don't forgive insults."

"Do you remember the way she flirted with Dale," I asked. "Tiffany had every reason to take her out. I know I felt like doing it when she flirted with you."

"Wait a minute," said Pat. "We're overlooking the most likely suspect. It's always the husband."

I shook my head. "No, John Ghent struck me as too passive."

Pat stepped behind me as I stood at the sink and put his arms around me. "And where were you on Tuesday night between 9:00 p.m. and midnight?"

"Why, officer," I replied, using the squeaky voice of a

movie chick, "I was home, all alone, so I don't really have an alibi."

"Hmm," he purred, as he squeezed me tighter. "I think you're resisting arrest. I'll have to take you into custody."

And with that, he picked me up and we headed for the bedroom.

Chapter 5

Thursday morning after breakfast I propped myself up on my futon to read and mark term papers for my new class, Modern Art. Throughout my first two years of teaching, I taught Art Appreciation, Art History I, and Art History II. By doing so, I had gotten enough students interested in art that a dozen or so would want to take a course that went into more depth. Last year, with a little arm-twisting, I got my department to approve the new course, and this semester, I enrolled eleven, just enough to satisfy the dean.

Since this was a course for juniors and seniors, I went beyond quizzes, exams and short reports and assigned a term paper. Throughout the semester, while walking them through the "-isms"—impressionism, symbolism, fauvism, expressionism, cubism, neo-classicism, etc.—I had also coached them on coming up with a topic, doing the research, and developing a thesis.

I read the term papers for nearly an hour and concluded they were varied to say the least. Some students took information from several sources, filled their papers with quotations and paraphrases, and said nothing about what they were trying to prove. Others praised a painter or a certain style and repeated that praise more and more forcefully in each succeeding paragraph. A few started with a mistaken definition of the chosen topic and went on to make ever wilder claims for its importance.

One paper was quite good. Elaine Wiltman had chosen to write about abstract expressionism, which was an ambitious choice. Most of my students avoided abstract art because it doesn't present a recognizable picture of something. Elaine started with the idea that this style was invented in response to social and economic conditions in the United States after the World War II. She said many painters stopped representing recognizable things and started working with abstract shapes and fields of color because the world wars had made the world unrecognizable. The evidence she presented may not have made her conclusion inevitable, but it was plausible.

I wondered how I had overlooked Elaine all semester in a class of eleven. Occasionally she asked a thoughtful question, but she'd never struck me as having this sort of insight.

I got to my office an hour before my first class to go through my routine for grading. I re-read the comments I had written on the papers and sorted them into piles for A, B, C, and D. Then I entered the grade for each paper on my spreadsheet for the class. Finally, I wrote the grade on the paper itself.

When I looked at the row on my spreadsheet for Elaine Wiltman, intending to enter an A for her paper, I noticed her grades on the quizzes were C's and D's. On the midterm essay exam, she earned a C-minus. That made me stop and look again at her paper and the comments I had written on it. No mistake: the paper really was top-notch. Had she soared so far above her earlier performance in the course by hard work and getting some tutoring from the Academic Skills Center? Or was there another explanation?

I finished entering the rest of the grades and marking the other papers, but decided not to hand them back to the class yet. That could wait until Friday.

As I looked over Elaine's paper once more, I had that prickly feeling that comes with facing sticky situations. I couldn't believe that a C-minus student had so quickly learned to write an A paper. But I couldn't simply tell her I didn't believe this paper was her own work. I needed evidence.

I spent the remaining time before class searching the

library's online databases for published articles on the origins of abstract expressionism that sounded like they might be similar to Elaine's paper, and ordered copies of a few.

If I ruled the world, I would have done further research on Tiffany's Picasso at lunchtime on Thursday. Instead, I convened the Gallery Advisory Committee, so we could settle on the fall exhibition and wrap things up for the year. No one brought lunch with them. I assumed the others preferred, as I did, not to eat in the cramped, windowless seminar room on the second floor of the Arts and Humanities Building.

"Here is the final information on Mira Robillard," I said as I passed around copies of a stapled packet to the members of the committee. "I think her watercolors are wonderful."

"Yes," said Greta Oswald, "we need some color."

Greta was consistently an advocate for color. On that spring day she wore a scarlet blouse with an orange plaid skirt and a lavender cardigan. She did not understand color, but she was definitely in favor of it.

Shirley Armstrong, associate professor of English, turned the pages of the handout. She had replaced Matt Dunkle on the committee a little over a year ago. Stopping at a photo of Robillard's picture of daffodils in a woodland setting, she said, "This reminds me, the daffodils are still blooming in that field beyond College Avenue. It also reminds me of Wordsworth. 'I wandered lonely as a cloud . . .'"

"We're talking about art, not literature, Shirley," said Greta.

"Thanks for mentioning that, Shirley," I said. "I'll have to take a walk out there and see them."

"I'd like to know what Bert thinks of these," said Shirley, grinning.

Bert Stemple, assistant professor of marketing, joined the faculty last fall when the School of Business opened. He was appointed to the committee to replace Millard Haflin, a retired professor of psychology, who passed away almost a year ago.

I'd been sorry to see Millard go. He had a way of speaking plainly that got to the heart of the matter.

A pleasant man in his forties, Bert had taken a break from business suits today, and was wearing a camel-hair jacket, brown slacks, and a pin-striped shirt with a dark tie. He must have gotten a haircut every week because I never saw a loose end around his ears or collar. His hair on top was so perfect around the edges that I wondered if he wore a toupee.

Shirley seemed to like Bert from the moment she met him at one of our meetings, and she often flirted with him. It seemed unlikely this would ever go anywhere, since she was more than ten years older than him. Ever the gentleman, Bert was pleasant but noncommittal with her.

"I agree with Nicole," said Bert. "They're beautiful."

"But the marketing, Bert," said Shirley, doubling down on her effort to woo him. "That's where you're so valuable to us."

"The gallery's brand is still coming into focus," said Bert. "As it does, we can identify different interest groups. After that, we can talk about a plan to reach out and bring more people into the exhibitions."

Shirley gaped like a fourteen-year-old. "That makes so much sense," she said with a wide smile.

"All right, then," I said. "With the committee's consent, I'll get a contract out to Mira Robillard and we'll schedule the exhibition for fall semester."

Greta chuckled and rolled her eyes. "Nicole, dear, we haven't even discussed this yet."

"Yes, we have, Greta. We discussed several artists last time and settled on Robillard."

"But," said Shirley, "what about the gallery's brand? It's . . . what did you say, Bert?"

"Coming into focus."

"Yes!" She gave him an especially warm smile.

"And that's just fine," I replied. "We can all watch as it comes into focus."

Shirley said, "But I'm just wondering if these

watercolors, lovely as they are, are helping to focus the gallery's brand. What do you think, Bert?"

"Well, yes, each additional exhibition brings it more and more into focus. You might say it fills in the picture a little more."

"That is so interesting," said Shirley, placing her elbow on the table, and resting her chin in her palm.

Bert looked at me with the beginnings of panic in his eyes. I had to do something to save him and spare myself from having to witness any more of Shirley's nauseating flattery. "Shirley," I said, "I think you could do us all a favor by looking back over our four exhibitions so far and giving us your impression of what kind of a gallery we're becoming."

"I'm not sure what you mean," she said.

"Send us all an email, describing the gallery's brand as you see it, giving examples of how each exhibit contributed."

Leaning forward, Shirley said, "I think Bert and I should meet to discuss that."

Bert was now glaring at me and he was beginning to perspire.

"No, Shirley," I said. "It would be best if any discussion took place with the full committee present. I was hoping your email would give us a starting point for that discussion."

"I don't think I feel up to doing that all by myself," she said, and I swear she seemed to be undressing him with her eyes.

"All right then," I said, "you and I can meet to discuss it next week. I'll send you an email."

She gave me a look that was noticeably cooler than the ones she had been sending Bert's way.

Hurrying to put this meeting out of its misery, I announced, "Hearing no objections to our selection of Robillard, I will proceed to get a contract out to her. We are adjourned. Thank you all for your service to the gallery. If I don't see you again, have a wonderful summer."

I hurried out of the seminar room, heading for my office,

feeling mildly depressed by having to manage the personalities of my committee. I would send Shirley an email, as I said I would. If she wrote back about a time to meet, I would take my time replying. With any luck that meeting would never take place.

By keeping the meeting short, I'd left myself just enough time to get to the Greenbrae Art Museum by two o'clock, which was when Sandra Carlini was expecting me. Since Saturday evening, I had been curious to add this small museum to my list of local favorites, which included the Columbus Museum of Art, the Cleveland Museum of Art, and the Cincinnati Art Museum. I also wanted to ask Sandra and Curtis for their impressions of Tiffany's Picasso.

As I made my third trip in six days up Route 35, stretches of the road started to look familiar. When I reached I-71, I would turn southwest to reach the town of Elbridge, instead of northeast as Pat and I had done the previous Saturday to get to Fairhaven for the Milman's dinner party.

I turned on the car's radio, and within a few minutes heard an hourly news report. I snapped to attention when I heard, "Police have arrested Tyrell Johnson of Wickwood in connection with the shooting death of Anne Ghent . . ." The report said nothing about a possible motive for the killing and nothing about how the police had located this suspect. I made a mental note to ask Sandra and Curtis if they had heard other reports.

Elbridge was built around a plaza, similar to the city of Sonoma, California, which I had often visited on trips to the wine country. This surprised me since Ohio does not have a history of Spanish influence as Northern California does. Yet Elbridge's plan was the same as Sonoma's with a courthouse, bronze statues, and other historic monuments in the middle of a green park that covered four square blocks. On the streets that bordered the park were a hotel and retail stores with offices above them. Passing these civic amenities on Church

Street, I saw three churches and a public library in a neighborhood of well-kept, large, old houses.

After passing through a section of smaller, newer houses, Church Street became Revere Road, which wound up a hillside. At the top I found the Greenbrae Art Museum in a late-Victorian house devoted to excess and ostentation. An octagonal tower topped with a witch's hat anchored one corner. A wide bay window with a gable above made up the opposite corner. A steep roof rose behind them both, promising vast spaces within.

I had learned from the museum's website that the house and the core of the art collection were the creations of Horace Oaks, a native of Elbridge, who went to Montana, made his fortune in mining, and returned to his home town in 1903. He married Lucy Revere, daughter of a local wealthy family, built a grand home, filled it with an art collection, and devoted himself to philanthropy for the remaining sixteen years of his life. Upon his death, all his property passed to his wife, and, since they had no heirs, she willed it all to a charitable foundation to benefit the town.

I drove past the front of the house and pulled into a graveled area, which, I assumed, was for parking though I saw no other cars there. Before getting out and walking back to the house, I sent Sandra a text to say I had arrived.

Chapter 6

By the time I climbed the steps to the roofed porch, which spanned the front of the house, Sandra Carlini was waiting at the front door.

"I hope you haven't opened just for me," I said.

"Not at all," she replied. "We were busy this morning, but things have tapered off this afternoon. Come on in."

The entry hall presented the visitor with a grand staircase and a corridor that led to the back of the house. On the right, through an archway, was a large parlor. To the left was a pair of smaller parlors, the first of which had a large bay window. Here they had set up the ticket counter and informational displays for welcoming visitors. Behind the second parlor was the dining room.

"There are Queen Anne houses like this in San Francisco," I said.

"Is that where you're from?"

I nodded. "And these are wonderful spaces for displaying this work," I said as we walked through the parlors.

"Thank you," said Sandra. "I think Curtis made a very good choice to concentrate on the best parts of Oaks' collection: painters of the Barbizon school, the better genre painters, the Hudson river school. Anyone who wants to survey art history can go to Cincinnati. Here, they can get a detailed look at American and European painting of the middle and late 1800s."

We arrived in the last gallery and I admired pictures of dramatic events played out against simplified backdrops of forests and hills. "I don't know this artist."

"George Caleb Bingham," said Sandra. "In the mid-1800s, he made a career of these scenes of campaign gatherings and polling places in rural locations. He was no realist. He deliberately idealized the political process of the young nation and depicted the landscape as a Garden of Eden. He celebrates the idea of a nation of farmers deciding their own destiny."

"Now that you mention it, I have heard his name, but I hadn't thought he was important."

"For a long time, he was dismissed as a commercial artist, but recently the art market has taken another look at him. There have been a couple significant auctions in the past few years of his works and those of his contemporaries."

I had to laugh. "Sometimes the dealers tell the historians where to look, instead of the other way around."

Sandra smiled. "It's a two-way street."

I turned to another wall that featured scenes of African Americans in ragged clothes. "And whose work is this?"

"Eastman Johnson. He painted these scenes of the daily lives of slaves during the 1850s. He was for a long time dismissed as sentimental, but all that changed about twenty years ago when his masterpiece, *Negro Life at the South*, got a major re-evaluation. The iconography in that picture is a subtle and satirical look at American society before the Civil War."

"Do you have it here?"

"No. Too bad. It's owned by the New York Historical Society."

Glancing around the room, I said, "So apparently Oaks had a good eye."

Sandra shrugged. "He bought some good stuff; he also bought some stuff that's not so good. Probably he simply followed the suggestions of dealers to buy works that were popular. He had a big house, and he was in a hurry to fill it up."

We walked back out to the front hall.

"Let's go upstairs," said Sandra. "We're not yet using the bedrooms for exhibition—we're still remodeling—but you can see the offices. I think Curtis is up here."

As we went along the upstairs corridor, I could see they would easily double their exhibition space once the remodeling was finished.

Sandra walked through a doorway to a back bedroom, and said, "Curtis, Nicole is here. I've just been showing her the collection."

As I walked in, he came around his desk to shake my hand. He wore a suit and tie as he had Saturday evening. He was, as I remembered, a few inches taller than me and lightly built. "Thank you so much for visiting this afternoon. I know it's a drive for you."

"Well worth it," I replied.

He gestured to two chairs in front of his desk. "Sit down. We can chat for a few minutes, although I'm waiting for a phone call, and I'll have to take it when it comes."

"Oh. Is that today?" asked Sandra.

Curtis nodded.

"You'd better stay focused," she said. Turning to me, she asked, "Would you like some coffee or tea?"

"Tea would be fine."

She turned back to Curtis and said, "We'll wait for you in the kitchen."

As we walked back down the corridor to the stairs, Sandra said, "I forget if that phone call is from a foundation or from a donor. Either way, we need the support. It's costing a fortune to bring this old place up to code and make it welcoming to the public. We've still got a long way to go."

"I hadn't thought of that. You're not just in the art business. You're also in the historic house business."

She nodded. "And the entertainment business, and the education business, and soon we'll be in the restaurant business. As Curtis likes to point out, our visitors have to drive out into farm country, get off the freeway, and drive through town to get here. So, we have to make ourselves a destination. I'm sure he's right, but there are times when it all seems like too much."

"Speaking of driving through town, the plaza in Elbridge is really pretty."

"What is?" asked Sandra.

"The green park with the big old building in the middle and the statues."

"Oh! Courthouse Square. Yes. It's lovely."

"Are there other towns like that in Ohio?"

"There are a few, though I think they're more common in the South."

At the bottom of the stairs we turned down the hall and walked back to the kitchen, which still had some original details but showed signs of being upgraded in stages through the 1960s. Sandra put the kettle on and got out mugs, a selection of tea bags and a tin of cookies. We sat at a table in the middle of the room.

"On the way over, I heard a news report about the murder of Anne Ghent," I said.

"That's a terrible thing."

"It said the police have arrested someone from Wickwood. I don't know where that is."

Sandra frowned for a moment before saying, "Wickwood is a small town between here and Columbus. It's bordered by a creek on one side and by the town of Shawville on the other three sides. In other words, on a map, it looks like someone took a bite out of Shawville and decided to call it Wickwood, which is exactly what happened. Shawville is full of nice, large houses where people like the Ghents live, people who aren't as wealthy as the Milmans, but are quite well-off. Wickwood was Shawville's downtown until the 1940s, when the city drew a line around it and made it a separate town whose population happens to be seventy percent African-American."

"Is that legal?"

"Technically, there's no segregation in Shawville or in

Wickwood. In either town, anyone can buy a house anywhere they want. Practically speaking, it's segregation. So, if the news reports say police have arrested 'a Wickwood man,' that most likely means a black man."

Sandra put tea bags into our mugs and poured water from the kettle. I was glad for the momentary distraction since this information prompted at least half a dozen questions and I didn't know where to start. I was prevented from pursuing them by the arrival of Curtis.

"Good news," he said to Sandra. "We're in the running."

"Congratulations, Mr. Director."

He sat opposite me at the table and Sandra made him a cup of tea.

"It's just one grant, and we certainly need more, but it's an important one," he said, grinning.

Sandra sat with us and smiled at him. "You and Peter should go out for dinner tonight and celebrate."

Curtis glared at her.

Sandra looked confused, glanced at me, and turned back to him. "Nicole is from San Francisco. I don't think she's going to be shocked that you have a boyfriend."

"That isn't the point. Why bring it up? Are you now going to ask Nicole to keep it confidential? Is that your plan?"

Sandra shook her head. "Nicole isn't going to run around spreading gossip about you."

"Again, not the point. I would like to keep my personal life private, and stick to business when we're working. Is that so much to ask?"

Sandra said, "I'm sorry, Curtis," but it sounded like more like a complaint than an apology.

Curtis turned to me. "Excuse us for bickering in front of you. I don't want this to be an issue when I'm talking to potential donors."

"No need to apologize," I said. "I'm really impressed with what you're doing here. I'd never really thought about all the challenges that come with the donation of a historic house and an art collection."

He nodded. "Thank you. There are times when I'm glad I didn't know what I was getting myself into when I took this job."

I glanced at my watch. "I'll have to get back on the road in a few minutes, but I did want to ask you about something. Did either of you get a good look at that painting by Picasso that hangs over the fireplace in Tiffany Milman's drawing room?"

Both nodded.

"We've both seen it on previous visits," said Sandra.

"I did some reading on Picasso's late paintings, and I visited Tiffany again on Tuesday, partly so I could get another look at it. I have a feeling there's a problem with it, but I can't put my finger on it."

"I don't know a lot about Picasso's late paintings," said Curtis.

"I don't either," I said, "and really no one does. They're just beginning to become available to the public. I'm concerned about this one because it just doesn't seem to have that energy one associates with an artist of his caliber."

Sandra said, "Even great painters produce mediocre paintings. But, I know what you mean. I've never really liked that painting."

"Excuse me," said Curtis, glaring at Sandra, "It's not our job to curate private collections."

"That's not what I'm doing, Curtis." Sandra rolled her eyes as she said this. "Relax! We're just having a casual conversation with a colleague."

"You're jeopardizing everything I'm trying to accomplish." He got up from the table. "Thank you for visiting this afternoon, Nicole. I hope you'll come back soon. Please excuse me." He left.

Sandra waited to hear his footsteps on the stairs before saying, "Forgive him. He's under a lot of pressure right now, and it's making him overreact."

"Don't worry about it," I said as I got up. "I should be going. Thanks for spending time with me this afternoon. This was great."

Sandra saw me off and I drove back through town to the freeway.

As I settled in for the hour-long drive back to campus, I felt a nagging irritation about the conclusion of my visit to Greenbrae. Thinking over our conversation in the kitchen, I kept coming back to the moment when Sandra told Curtis, "You and Peter should go out for dinner tonight and celebrate," and Curtis made it clear he preferred not to be out at work.

This reminded me of the moment at the dinner party on the previous Saturday when Tiffany invited the "ladies" to come with her to the drawing room, and also called on Curtis to see a new addition to her collection. As he walked to the door, Anne Ghent remarked that he was "just one of the girls."

In other circumstances, such a comment would have been a mildly humorous way of easing any tension that might arise from one man joining a group of women in a social situation. But, in light of what I'd just learned, Anne's remark, delivered at a gathering of wealthy people, might have felt like a threat to his ongoing efforts to attract support for Greenbrae.

As Sandra said, he was under a lot of pressure. Was the pressure great enough that Anne's remark would have motivated him to seek revenge? When I asked myself that question, the reason for my discomfort became clear. A few minutes earlier, I might have been sitting across the table from a murderer.

Once I had thought it and said it aloud to myself in the privacy of my car, it sounded ridiculous. The thought of a well-dressed, well-educated man like Curtis somehow getting a gun and lurking in a parking lot to shoot and kill someone who taunted him seemed at first laughable. But if I laughed at that possibility, I was joining everyone else in turning to Wickwood for likely suspects, a mental habit that was as morally corrupt as it was convenient.

Since I couldn't stop thinking about this, I decided to search online for news stories about the murder of Anne Ghent and the arrest of Tyrell Johnson. At least I had to find out who he was and why he was at the mall two nights ago.

Chapter 7

When I got home from my visit to Greenbrae Art Museum, I checked my calendar and was glad to see I had nothing planned for tomorrow except my classes at eleven and one. I could feel the school year winding down. There would be another frenzy of activity as we approached final exams, and once the year ended I would dive into research for an article on one of our recent exhibits, but for now there was a lull. I hadn't talked to Pat about plans for the weekend. Maybe we would spend a night in Cincinnati or Columbus.

Filling my backpack for tomorrow morning, I came across the articles I had downloaded about the origins of abstract expressionism. They reminded me I had to make a decision about Elaine Wiltman's paper so I could hand back papers in tomorrow morning's Modern Art class. I chose the article with the most likely title, read the introduction, and recognized it as the source of her paper. Clearly, she had used this article but had not mentioned it in the body of the paper and had not added a footnote or endnote to acknowledge it.

This was frustrating, but not unusual. Many students thought research meant finding something on the internet and putting it in their paper, sometimes simply by cutting and pasting. Looking over Elaine's paper, I saw she mostly had summarized the article, though there were sections of close paraphrase.

I had explained to the students that a research paper that reported what others had already said without adding anything original would be graded C, or maybe B if it was well-written, which Elaine's was. But before I could write that grade on the paper and hand it back to her, she would have to acknowledge her source.

Instead of writing a grade on her paper, I attached a sticky note that read, "See me after class."

On my way to class Friday morning, I stopped by the espresso bar, which anchored one corner of the plaza in front of the new business building. It was essentially a glass house with a free-standing service counter in the middle. I had become fond of picking up a latte and taking it to my office, so much so that I allowed myself to indulge on Mondays and Fridays only.

As I stood in line, I gazed out the back wall of the cafe and took in the new home of the School of Business. Its mostly glass facade allowed the passerby to look into the atrium at the center of the building and see everyone moving between classrooms, lecture halls, and offices.

There was nothing else like it on our little campus. The original buildings from the 1920s were collegiate gothic. The Student Center was early shopping mall, and the Arts and Humanities Building, where I had my office and taught, was in the international style.

I glanced toward the head of the line at the man ordering and recognized Bert Stemple by his perfect hair. After placing my own order, I caught up with him at the end of the counter where we waited for our drinks.

"I can't tell you how glad I am we now have this place," I said.

Bert deadpanned. "Without it, the university couldn't have hired faculty for the School Business."

I smiled. "Thank you for raising our standards."

He smiled back. "Thank you for bailing me out at our meeting yesterday."

"Don't mention it."

He shook his head. "I don't usually get tongue-tied like

that, but I was caught off-guard."

"Shirley was out of line. Now that I think of it, if a man had done the same thing to a woman on the faculty, she'd have filed a complaint."

He shook it off. "Nothing to worry about. Seriously though, I'd be happy to help with the marketing for the gallery. When you have a sense of how you'd like the gallery to grow, just let me know."

"Thank you, Bert. I'll do that."

He picked up his drink and headed for the Business Building.

As I waited for mine, I faced a new set of questions. Up to then, I'd focused on recruiting good artists and researching their backgrounds. I hadn't thought about how I'd like the gallery to grow. It felt good to be challenged by a new colleague, but I'd have to put off thinking about marketing until summer . . . or maybe fall.

I waited until the end of my Modern Art class to hand back their papers. Otherwise, the students would have spent the class period thinking about their grades. Also, after class Elaine Wiltman could find out right away why she got "See me after class" instead of a grade.

She waited in her seat while the others left the room, some pausing to ask me questions. When they were gone she came forward, holding up her paper with my sticky note showing. "Hi," she said with a smile. "What's up?"

"Good paper," I said, as I pulled the relevant article out of my backpack. "I can see you used this as a source. So, I just need you to acknowledge it, either in your introduction or in an endnote."

She scowled as she took the article from my hand. When she had scanned the first page, she looked up and said, "I don't understand."

"It's okay to use sources like this, so long as you tell the reader you're doing it."

"But I didn't," she said.

I almost couldn't believe she was denying it. "Elaine, your first paragraph about the origins of abstract expressionism is a paraphrase of the introduction to this article. The examples you use to prove your point are the same ones used in this article. In your conclusion, there's a sentence that is identical to one at the end of this article except for three-word substitutions. So, obviously your paper is based on this article, and that's fine, but you have to acknowledge it as your source. That's what I'm trying to teach you."

Her cheeks were flushed and her eyes were searching the floor as if looking for something to say. She dropped the article on the table next to my backpack and said, "I don't know what you're talking about. I just read the textbook and wrote my paper."

I felt sorry for her. Something was making her think she had to lie her way out of the situation.

"I'll make this easy on you," I said. "You can use your pen right now to add the word 'Sources' to the last page of your paper and add the author's name, the title of the article, and so on. That's all you need to do. This is just so we're clear on the need to acknowledge sources."

"No," she said and hurried out of the room.

I was stunned. I couldn't understand why she would deny something so obvious when there was no disadvantage for her in acknowledging it. Fortunately, she had the weekend to think about it. I hoped she would talk to some friends who might explain to her this was no big deal. With any luck, she would show up on Monday with the acknowledgement in place and I could give her a grade.

Back in my office, I munched on some salad with chopped egg and toast while leaning back in my chair and looking out over the wooded hillside that descended from the back of the Arts and Humanities Building. This view was the architect's gift to the faculty.

I kept a windbreaker in my office so I could hang it on the

hook I had added just above the little window in my office door. That way the passing students couldn't glance in, see me eating, decide I wasn't doing anything important, and pop in to tell me what they had planned for the weekend and ask, "Doesn't that sound cool?" There was plenty of time for that when I wasn't eating.

Alone with the view, I marveled at the pale green blush of the budding trees. Within a month that would turn into a heavy green canopy. Here and there, at the edges of the forest and in clearings, were smaller trees blooming in white and pink.

This was my third spring in the Appalachian foothills of Ohio, and I still had to remind myself that those flowering trees were native species. This was a powerful lesson for a girl from San Francisco where there are no native trees. When Europeans arrived, the peninsula was sand dunes covered with grasses. Every tree in my hometown was put there by the hand of Man, but Nature was the gardener here.

I finished my lunch and, before getting back to the business of preparing for my one-o'clock class, sent Pat a text: Dinner, your place, stir-fry chicken and veg?

That evening, as we worked together chopping things to go into the wok, I told Pat about my bewildering conversation with the student who preferred to tell an obvious lie, rather than add a note to the end of her paper.

He agreed her behavior made no sense and asked, "Did you actually show her a copy of the article?"

"Yes. That's how I started, and I told her it was okay to use it as a source. I think I even complimented her on it."

"And what was her first reaction?"

"She seemed confused."

"About why you were bringing it up? Or did she just not recognize the article?"

I couldn't quite remember her reaction. "Could have been either," I said, "although I think I was pretty clear about why I was bringing it up. Now that I think of it, she stared at the first page of the article for a while before she said anything."

Pat nodded. "She probably had never seen it before."

"Then how did she write her paper based on it?"

"She didn't write the paper."

"Then how . . . ?" My brain froze.

"Someone wrote it for her and based it on the article but didn't tell her that," said Pat.

I was so stunned I had to put down my knife and step back from the counter. "How did I not see that?"

"Is this the first time it's happened to you?"

"I've had students hand in work that wasn't their own—a couple when I was a grad student—but those were obvious because they didn't bother to rewrite it in their own words or because they picked an article that was mostly irrelevant to the course."

Pat popped a slice of green pepper into his mouth and chewed before replying. "So, this was a better class of cheating. Your student probably found someone who writes well, maybe someone who knows something about art, and went over the assignment with them. That person wrote the paper either for pay or for a favor in return. Your student may have read the paper but didn't ask what, if anything, it was based on."

"But, when I showed her the article, she could have covered up the whole scheme just by saying, 'Oh, sorry, I forgot to name my source,' and writing it on the last page. I told her she could do that."

"Yes, that would have worked, but, since she probably had never seen that article, she wasn't thinking clearly. She followed her first instinct, which was to deny everything."

I stood there feeling stupid for not seeing what Pat was describing. I also felt depressed, thinking of the energy I had wasted trying to turn this into a learning experience for Elaine Wiltman.

Pat glanced at me and at the chicken lying on the cutting board where I had been working. "We'll have to put that in the wok first." He put some oil in the wok and turned on a burner.

I stepped back to the counter and started cutting. "Now what do I do?" I asked. "If she comes back on Monday, and says, 'Here you go. I added that end note,' do I accuse her of cheating?"

Pat pursed his lips before saying, "That might be tricky since you've already told her she can do that."

"But she denied knowing anything about the article, and refused to acknowledge it. How could she explain that?"

"To whom would she have to explain it?"

"To me."

"What if she says, 'Sorry. I was confused,' and hands you a paper with the source noted on the last page."

"That would obviously be bogus. I can't accept the paper now."

"I'll remind you again: You already told her she could do that."

The oil was starting to smoke. Pat pointed at the chicken, and at the wok, and said, "Let's make ourselves a nice dinner and enjoy it."

He went into the dining room, and I heard him putting plates and silverware on the table. I dumped the chicken in the wok, added seasonings, and kept stirring. As I got into a rhythm of scooping ingredients out of the wok and putting others in and combining the flavors, I felt myself pulling back from the knotty problem of handling a student's dishonesty and instead embracing the immediate prospect of enjoying a meal with the man I loved.

And enjoy it we did, while discussing what we might do when we went up to Columbus the next day and where we might stay overnight before coming back on Sunday.

This being Friday, we allowed ourselves an extra drop of wine and were just sitting back to sip it when my phone rang.

Chapter 8

I wondered if my parents in San Francisco were calling as I trotted to the living room and fished my phone out of my purse, but the phone's screen said, "Private Number." I had never gotten a robocall that announced itself that way, so I answered.

"Professor Noonan, this is John Ghent. I hope you don't mind my calling you. I got your number from Tiffany Milman."

"Hello, John. No, that's fine. And, may I say, I'm very sorry for your loss. Pat and I were very sad when we heard of Anne's death."

Of course, I felt terrible saying that, considering how we joked about it Wednesday evening, as if her being killed were something that happened in a murder mystery, but what else could I say?

"Thank you," said John. "I appreciate that. I'm calling to ask a favor."

"Of course, John, anything I can do."

"Anne bought some paintings over the years, some of them rather expensive. They're really more suitable for her taste than mine. I'm thinking about selling them, but I don't really know anything about them. I'm pretty sure we have all the receipts, so I could get in touch with the galleries where she bought them, but I don't know if that's the best way to go. Frankly, I'm finding it difficult to think straight about anything these days. I don't know where to start."

"How can I help?"

"Would you come to the house and take a look at them? I know that's a lot to ask, and I would insist on paying you a consulting fee. I'm sure you would know at a glance whether or not these paintings are valuable, and perhaps you could advise me on the best way to sell them."

"John, I don't mind coming to look at them. I wouldn't charge a fee. Service to the university and the wider community is part of my job description. I would be happy to tell you what I know about the paintings. I don't have experience buying and selling works of art, but I can find out what your options are."

"Thank you. You've taken a great weight off my shoulders."

"When would you like me to visit?"

"At your convenience. I'm taking some time off work, so I can make my own schedule."

"May I call you back later this evening to set up a time?"

"Of course. Or just send me a text saying when you'd like to visit. We live . . . sorry, I live in Shawville. I'll send you my address in an email."

I offered my condolences once more, said goodbye, and hung up.

I returned to the dining room to find that Pat had cleared the table and retired to the kitchen to wash dishes. I caught up with him and said, "That was a strange phone call."

"Who was it?"

"John Ghent."

Pat stopped washing and gave me his full attention.

"He called to ask me to help him sell Anne's paintings."

"She had her own paintings?"

"He said she bought them over the years, and they were not to his taste, so, yeah, I guess they were hers more than his."

Pat shrugged and went back to washing.

I picked up a towel and started drying. "Doesn't it seem strange that he's selling her paintings only—how long has it been?—three days after her death?"

"Not especially," said Pat. "There's no such thing as normal when a spouse dies, let alone when she's murdered. Some people react by keeping themselves busy with all kinds of chores, even ones that aren't urgent. That way they can postpone feeling the loss."

"Keeping busy I can see, but why is he so eager to eliminate all traces of her from their house?"

"We don't know that he is. He might be focusing on the paintings simply because he doesn't like them, as he said. When it comes to her clothes, her jewelry, and other personal possessions, he may wait a while, a long time even. For now, maybe this just gives him something to do."

"I suppose. Still, something about it bothers me. It seems cold and calculating, almost as if he had planned to do this when she was gone."

"Seriously, Nicole, don't make too much out of this."

I stacked the plates and put them into the kitchen cabinet. "I'm supposed to get back to him about when to visit his house and take a look at the paintings."

"Is he in a hurry for this?"

"No, but I kind of am. I have to admit I'm curious about seeing another private collection. I'm also curious about what kind of house they live in. They are country-club people, after all."

"I wouldn't expect anything on the scale of the Milmans'. I don't think there are many around like that."

"No, but still . . ." I wasn't sure how to bring up what I was thinking.

"Do you want to get this done this weekend?" he asked.

"Yeah, I do."

"Do you want to do it tomorrow?"

"If you don't mind."

"I don't. I have some chores to do anyway, and I need to squeeze in another workout. We can still go up to Columbus for the day on Sunday."

"Okay. Can I sleep over tonight?"
"Of course."
"And I still get to sleep over Saturday night?"
"Of course. Saturday is always our night."
"Mm. You're the best."

I set out from campus around eight thirty Saturday
morning so I could arrive at John Ghent's house in Shawville
by ten. Although I was happy to develop donors for the college
and to perform community service, this was my third trip to
the area southwest of Columbus in five days. Altogether those
three trips would cost me an extra tank of gas. If this kept up, I
would have to see about getting some reimbursement from the
university.

From the freeway I took a six-lane highway through a
cluster of strip malls. A few miles past the exit which led
toward Fairhaven, the highway reduced to four lanes and then
to two by the time I saw a marker made of fieldstone and
timbers marking the entrance to Shawville. From there on I
drove on winding roads just wide enough for two cars to pass.
Apparently, Shawville did not encourage the free flow of
traffic.

It was a neighborhood of big new houses surrounded by
big old trees. No two houses were alike. Each had a different
configuration of roofline, dormers, garage-door placement,
porches, and window size. Yet in its relentless variety there
was a sameness to the neighborhood. The word "custom"
applied equally to all.

I found the *cul-de-sac* named in John's address and
parked in his driveway next to a car nearly twice the length of
my economy car. I would have needed a step-stool to get into
it and a booster seat to see over the steering wheel.

As Pat predicted, the Ghents' house was not on the scale
of the Milmans', but was impressive nonetheless. I rang the
doorbell and waited.

Looking around the *cul-de-sac*, I saw no one stirring, and didn't even hear a dog barking. If anyone was doing anything outdoors on this fine spring day, they were doing it behind their houses, alone, in their private clearings in the woods.

I remembered John as a thin man with leathery skin and a stooped posture. When he came to the door, he seemed all that and worse. The strain of the past four days had weakened him. As he opened the door and greeted me by name, he smiled with his eyes but could not lift the corners of his mouth. He wore a white dress shirt and trousers that probably belonged to a suit with well-shined loafers, which gave the impression that he had no business to dress for but couldn't find a sport shirt and slacks.

"Good morning, John," I said. "How are you?"

He shrugged. "Let's go through to the family room."

From the front hall, we turned down a hallway that took us to a room with a high ceiling and full-length windows opening to the yard and woods behind the house. A leather sectional sofa was arranged to take full advantage of the view.

"Can I get you anything?" he asked.

"No, thank you," I said.

He pulled up his cuff and looked at his watch. "A little early, I guess."

We sat in two reclining chairs by the window. My feet did not touch the floor.

His eyes settled on something across the room but it seemed his mind was far away.

"I heard the police have decided to bring charges against the man they arrested," I said.

A spasm went through his arms and his hands became fists. "We aren't safe from those people in our own community, our own homes." This was said just above a whisper.

I had to wonder if in another context he might include Asians when he said, "those people." Since the thought of justice did nothing to comfort him, I asked, "Will there be a memorial service?"

He stared at me, startled by the question. "Of course. Next Thursday. I . . . oh, I see . . . I'm so sorry. I must not have sent you an announcement."

"That's alright."

"You met her so recently, but . . . you knew her. Of course, you should be there. Only if you wish to . . . you and . . . I'm sorry . . . the other professor who came with you to the dinner party."

"Pat Gillespie."

"Yes. I'll send the information to your email address at the college, if that's alright."

"Of course," I said.

His eyes drifted to the wooded scene outside the windows. His shoulders slumped even further.

Afraid he might fall asleep, I asked, "You said there are some paintings?"

He glanced at me, surprised. "Oh. Yes, of course. In the library."

Chapter 9

We left the family room and went down the corridor to a pleasant corner room on the front of the house. Windows on two sides gave good light for viewing the art on the two interior walls. At a glance I saw a nice collection of half a dozen paintings, less spectacular than Tiffany's but fine all the same.

"Are you sure you won't have something?" he asked.

"No, thank you."

"Alright then, if you'll excuse me for a moment, I'll be right back."

One of Anne's paintings was of a cafe scene in springtime, judging by the blossoms on the vines. The style was definitely impressionism, and the subject recalled Renoir, but this painter's touch was heavier. The signature was sketchy, but I think it said "Johansen." I jotted the name in a little notebook along with a brief description and estimate of the size.

I did the same with the other paintings before focusing on the one that had caught my eye the moment I walked in. It was a Picasso, less than half the size of Tiffany's. It depicted a mother and child. Both were nude and the mother sat with her knees apart so that her genitals and anus were visible. Their faces were white discs with simplified features painted on them.

As I had learned, the crude, explicit detail and the cartoonish exaggeration were typical of his late work. Like Tiffany's Picasso, the whole thing felt forced.

I was starting to write in my notebook when I heard John Ghent behind me.

"These can all be sold. They were hers. Some of them are nice, but they just don't mean much to me."

I noticed he was holding a tall glass of what looked like orange juice over ice.

"They are nice," I said. "Do you recall where she bought them?"

"These," he said, gesturing toward four small paintings to the right, "all came from different galleries here in Columbus. I made copies of the invoices for you." He handed me a manila envelope.

"Thank you." I took it and tucked it under my arm.

"That one, she bought when we were on vacation in upstate New York," he said, pointing to a large one on the left. "And that one," he pointed to the Picasso, "came from a gallery in New York City."

"Do you recall which one?"

"Yes, the Redburn Gallery. The invoice is in there," he said, nodding toward the manila envelope. He took a long drink of the orange juice and followed it with a deep sigh.

"It's easily the most expensive," I said.

He smiled as he settled himself on a small sofa, leaned back, and crossed his legs. "I'd like to get top dollar for these. Should I take them all to one dealer or will I have to sell one here and another one there?"

"I suspect there's quite a range of value here. Some dealers concentrate in the higher end of the market, while some serve a broader clientele. I'll ask some friends."

"I don't want this to take up too much of your time," he said, making an earnest attempt at courtesy.

"This won't take long," I said. "A few phone calls. Would you mind if I took a photo of the Picasso?"

"Be my guest." He waved his arm to indicate I was free to photograph any and all of the paintings. He now seemed to be enjoying our visit.

After I took a picture with my cell phone, he got up from the couch. He had finished his drink, and now stood straighter and had more color in his cheeks. "Can I offer you some lunch?" he asked. "Now that I think of it, we could run over to the club for a bite." He checked his watch. "It's a little early but it's Saturday, so I'm sure they'll be serving."

"Thank you, but I have to get back to campus," I said. "So much to do at the gallery." Actually, I had nothing to do at the gallery, but I couldn't imagine going with him for lunch when he was both emotionally fragile and on his way to being drunk.

"Alright, then," he said and waved me toward the corridor.

As I walked toward the front hall, I saw a door open that had been closed when we walked to the library. I glanced in, as I went by, and saw that it was nicely furnished as an office, but had file folders strewn across the desk top and cardboard file boxes all over the floor and even perched on the seats of the chairs and sofa.

We said our goodbyes, and I got in my little car and drove back out to the highway.

As I started on my way, I thought about how I would do what I had promised John Ghent. It wouldn't be difficult. Two members of my department were painters and would be familiar with local galleries. They could tell me who to talk to. Also, Sandra Carlini must have been involved in putting together Greenbrae's auction and would probably be willing to put me in touch with whoever they used. I was fairly sure I could have an answer for John within a few days.

More puzzling was the appearance of one very expensive painting in Anne's otherwise mid-to-low-price collection. The more I thought about it, the more eager I was to get home, open that manila envelope, and take a look at the receipt for Anne's Picasso. Like Tiffany's Picasso, Anne's had been purchased from the Redburn Gallery in New York, both paintings showed all the characteristics of Picasso's late work, and both lacked the vitality one associates with a master. That seemed like a lot of coincidences.

However, if both paintings had the same provenance, all this became more believable. If, for instance, both paintings came from the same owner, and that owner was the heir of a person who received both paintings from Picasso himself, then everything made sense. Picasso might have dashed off a pair of paintings with minimal inspiration and given them to a friend. Decades later, the heir needed to raise cash and sold them both through the same dealer. Provenance should be easy to check. A phone call to the dealer should do it.

Instead of turning left to go back through the shopping malls to the freeway, I turned right. Directions on my phone told me that was the way to Wickwood. I wanted to see the city with a majority black population that, on a map, looked like someone had taken a bite out of Shawville. I wanted to know who John Ghent was talking about when he said, "those people."

Before leaving home that morning, I'd read news accounts of the arrest of Tyrell Johnson. On the night of the murder, he finished his shift at a store that sold everything for the home and garden and walked to his car. He saw an ambulance and police car nearby and walked over to see what was going on. When officers questioned him, Johnson said he was leaving work and pointed to his car to back up his explanation. The officers searched his car and found a handgun in the glove compartment.

The road I was on wound past some older shopping centers and bordered on developments of smaller houses, the kind that went up fast after the World War II. I drove across a steel truss bridge and passed a sign saying, "Welcome to Wickwood."

Two-story brick buildings typical of small older towns in Ohio lined both sides of the street. This town was noticeably smaller than Elbridge, where I had gone to visit the Greenbrae Art Museum, and even smaller than Blanton, the little town near my university. The business district of Wickwood extended only one block in each direction, and the storefronts were filled with the usual assortment of clothing shops, hair salons, and fast-food franchises.

Having passed through the town's only commercial intersection, I drove another block and came to a fine two-story school building, built of red brick and trimmed with limestone, sitting on a few acres of lawn, surrounded by an iron fence. The large mullioned windows and sparse gothic ornaments suggested it was built in the early twentieth century.

Turning on the street next to the school, I entered a pleasant neighborhood of mostly two-story, wooden houses, set several yards back from the street, and a few yards from each other. Mature trees next to the curbs shaded the street and sidewalks. On a few of the porches that spanned the front of nearly every house, people sat out, reading, conversing, and keeping an eye on the neighborhood. Children rode bikes on sidewalks or in the streets, depending on their ages. In one driveway, some teenage guys shot hoops.

As I looked around this pleasant neighborhood going about its Saturday-morning business, it was hard to imagine one of these men going to his job at a distant mall, shooting a woman he had never met, and taking whatever was in her purse. It was possible, of course, but it was also possible that Tyrell Johnson had been arrested because folks in this county including law enforcement had gotten used to thinking of Wickwood as the neighborhood where murderers come from.

As I drove more than an hour back to my university, I felt sad about the situation—Shawville and Wickwood—and I felt helpless. Angered by John Ghent's racist remark, I considered telling him I couldn't help him after all, but that would have seemed like kicking a man when he was down. I decided to be kind to him and trust that kindness would make the world a better place.

I also decided to call the officer leading the murder investigation according to that news story, Detective Brian Murphy. Perhaps he had sufficient evidence to keep Tyrell

Johnson in jail. But, since I had my suspicions about Curtis Diaz, I could at least let him know Johnson wasn't the only credible suspect.

Chapter 10

When I got home I decided to get the easy stuff out of the way first. In the manila envelope, I found a receipt from the Redburn Gallery for a painting by Picasso. The price was $625,000. I guessed that was easily five times the value of any other painting in Anne's collection.

I sent Sandra Carlini an email saying I was helping John Ghent get ready to sell some paintings and wanted to know which auction house Greenbrae used and whether it might be willing to work with an individual to sell a few pieces.

As for galleries, I decided to wait until Monday or Tuesday when I would see my colleagues in our department's offices.

I had just started an online search for the Redburn Gallery's website when my phone rang. It was Sandra Carlini.

"Hi, Nicole, did you get my email? I just sent it."

I clicked over to my email window. "Yeah, I see it, but I haven't read it yet."

"Don't bother. Basically, I was brushing you off by mentioning the names of some well-known auction houses and suggesting you call them. I did that because Curtis has a policy of not sharing information about our auction."

"Really? Why?"

"Down the line, we're going to apply for accreditation with the American Association of Museums. They frown on museums selling off parts of their collections, so we're trying to control that information."

"Alright. Sorry, I didn't mean to pry."

"Not at all. I don't mind telling you about it. I just didn't want to put it in an email that came to my Greenbrae address. It's not that Curtis monitors my emails; I just thought it was better not to put my answer on the museum's email server."

"I see. Well, thanks for calling me."

"No problem. So, you're helping John Ghent?"

"John called me on Friday and said he wanted to sell some paintings because Anne collected them, and they meant more to her than they do to him. Apparently, she bought them all through galleries, and I suppose he should just take them back to the same galleries, but I thought I would check with you about how auction houses work."

"Definitely he should look into it. Auction prices can go through the roof if the bidding gets competitive."

"He has eight paintings. Would an auction house be interested in a collection that small?"

"They might be. I have a file of materials from our sale I could go over with you. Do you want to meet?"

"Sure. Let me look at my calendar and see when I have time to get over your way."

"Actually, I was thinking I would do the driving this time. You made the trip over here on Thursday, so that only seems fair. Plus, since Curtis is a bit secretive on this subject, I'd rather not meet at Greenbrae or even in Elbridge. It's a small town."

"There's a nice coffee house in Chillicothe. I've only been there once, so we're not likely to run into anyone I know either."

"Perfect."

I gave her the address of Klein's on North Paint Street. We decided to meet at two o'clock the next afternoon and said goodbye.

Then I remembered that Pat had said we would make a day trip up to Columbus on Sunday. Either I had to call Sandra back and reschedule, or I had to renegotiate my plans with my man.

Renegotiating looked like the way to go, so I hopped in my car to make a quick trip to Blanton and buy a nice bottle of wine to have with dinner at his house.

When I got back from Blanton, it was still early for preparing dinner, but I put the slightly-more-expensive-than-usual bottle of Chardonnay in my backpack along with a book on CGI animation and walked over to Pat's house anyway. If, as I expected, he was in his study, in a trance, analyzing data on his computer screen, I could stretch out on the living room couch and read until he was again ready for human interaction.

As I stepped up onto his front porch, I noticed the cool breeze that often came with evening had not yet come up. The thought of getting comfortable in one of the Adirondack chairs appealed, but when I glanced in the living room window I saw Pat running the vacuum cleaner. I've always found it enjoyable to watch a man do housework, so I just stood there.

Within a minute, he glanced at the window. Even at a distance I could see those green eyes sparkling. He shut off the vacuum and came to the door. "Coming in?" he asked.

"No. Just enjoying the show."

"Get in here, before the neighbors get suspicious."

"I think we're way past that point," I said as I slid past him into the living room and dropped my backpack on a chair.

He wrapped his arms around me and made me feel better than I had all day. I paid him back with a smooch.

I perched on the arm of the couch while he packed up the vacuum cleaner.

"How did it go with John Ghent?" he asked.

"Fine. Anne bought some nice paintings, but, you were right, nothing like Tiffany's collection."

"So, you've done your good deed?"

"Not quite yet, I have to check with some people so I know what to tell him about working with galleries or using an auction house."

"Keep notes on all this, or maybe write yourself a memo

each time you do one of these, so you can document all this service to the university when you apply for promotion."

That was obviously the practical thing to do, yet it had never occurred to me. One could not get promoted or tenured simply by saying, "I taught my classes and I published these articles." One also had to tell a story about how one was useful to the school. Thinking it over, I was pretty sure I could review my calendar for the past three years, and reconstruct convincing documentation, but from now on I would keep notes as I went along. Applying for my first promotion was less than a year away. One more thing for the to-do list.

"Thanks for that suggestion," I said. "I'm concerned about John. When I got there he seemed weak, confused, unable to concentrate . . ."

Pat glanced up at me. "He has just lost his wife in an especially horrible way."

"I understand, but there's more. He kept asking if I wanted something to drink. When I started taking notes on the paintings, he went to the kitchen and came back with a glass of orange juice with ice in it. By the time he had finished drinking it, it was like he'd had a personality transplant. He chatted about the paintings and how and where Anne bought them. He was very gracious about asking me for a favor and offered to pay me. He even invited me to have lunch with him at 'the club.'"

Pat nodded. "Obviously, there was some vodka in that orange juice."

"I'm sure you're right."

"He may be killing the pain. A lot of people drink more after they lose someone. With any luck he'll get counseling or some other kind of support and work through the pain rather than medicating it with alcohol or something else."

"Is it possible he was showing his true self?"

Pat thought about that for a moment. "I'm not sure what you mean."

"It wasn't as if he started giving away secrets. He said

pretty much what he had said on the phone with me, but his attitude was different. As he talked about selling Anne's paintings, he seemed to be enjoying the transaction. When he handed me a folder full of invoices, I half-expected him to say, 'It's been a pleasure doing business with you.'"

Pat nodded. "It's possible he was feeling that euphoria that comes with the first drink."

"But then, as we walked out, I glanced into his study. He had left the door open. There were boxes everywhere. I wondered if he was packing to move or to put some things in storage."

"His wife's death may have provoked him to clean house . . . make a fresh start."

"Or her death may have been the beginning of his fresh start."

"Meaning what?"

"Maybe he killed her."

Pat stared out the window for a few seconds. "I really wouldn't make too much out of what you saw. We try to see patterns in people's actions—especially we psychologists. We love to talk about things like 'the five stages of grief,' but in reality there are no rules about how people behave. Vague tendencies, perhaps, but human behavior is an endless mystery."

"By the way, John Ghent said there's a memorial service planned for next Thursday. I think we should go."

"We only met them a week ago."

"True, but we could still support someone going through a difficult time."

Pat looked confused. "You just said you suspect him of murder. Now you want to support him in his hour of need?"

I batted my eyelashes. "As you said, human behavior is an endless mystery."

Pat smiled. "Seriously, why do you want to attend?"

"I imagine all the people from the dinner party will be there. It would be interesting to see them together in a different context."

He folded his arms and looked smug. "So, really, you want to go so you can observe their interactions and make deductions about their motives?"

"Me? Admit it: You've thought about whether one of them could have killed her."

"Of course. We talked about that when we first heard she'd been killed. But I'm not making plans to infiltrate their social circle so I can snoop on them."

"Neither am I. Although, now that you mention it, maybe someone should look into their motives."

"What do you mean?"

"Have you been following news reports about the investigation?"

"I've seen a couple of stories online."

"The police have arrested a man named Tyrell Johnson from a town called Wickwood."

Pat shrugged. "I guess I missed that."

"I drove through Wickwood on my way back to campus this afternoon. It was Shawville's black neighborhood until someone decided to draw a line around it and call it a separate town. So, basically, the police found a black guy to arrest."

"It's also possible they have some evidence against this man."

"In an ideal world, that would be true. Anyway, the memorial service is Thursday afternoon. Are you going with me or do I have to get another date?"

"Well, when you put it that way, I guess I'll have to go with you so some other guy doesn't jump my claim."

I pulled the bottle of wine from my backpack and handed it to him. "I brought this to have with dinner tonight," I said, as casually as I could.

He studied the label for a moment. "Is there anything you want to tell me?"

"What do you mean?"

"This is a nice bottle of wine. If you're trying to soften

me up for something, you've succeeded."

I put my arms around him and kissed his chin. "About that day-trip to Columbus tomorrow: I have a problem."

Chapter 11

Chillicothe was like many of the towns I'd visited in southern Ohio, only bigger. It had more intersections and some grand buildings from when it was the state capitol in the 1800s. Its neighborhoods fanned out wider and looked better because it was sustained by a paper mill. But it was the same kind of town: red-brick buildings with stores at street level and offices above.

Klein's Coffee Shop occupied one of those storefronts on North Paint Street and had room for dozens of people. Since Chillicothe was the county seat, there were law offices up and down the street, and I imagined on weekday mornings Klein's must be full of lawyers in pin-striped suits. On this Sunday afternoon the town was quiet and there were only three tables occupied. I got myself a latte and could not resist the blueberry crumble, which looked like it was made locally.

I had no sooner sat down at a table by the front window than Sandra came in, dropped her coat and tote bag on a chair, handed me a file folder, and said, "I'll be right back." She was dressed down for Sunday—jeans, sneakers, and sweater—as I was.

Flipping through the folder, I saw some letters, printed announcements of past auctions including Greenbrae's, photocopied lists of policies, warnings, and disclaimers, and odds and ends including a take-out menu from a restaurant that, I assumed, must be near the auction house in New York. I took out my notebook and jotted down names, addresses, emails, and phone numbers.

Sandra came back with a bottle of cranberry juice, twisted the cap off, and took a swig. "This is kind of a cute place," she said, looking around the cafe. "I've never been to Chillicothe."

"Unless you're passing through on your way to Cardinal or Ohio U. in Athens there's nothing but farms out this way."

Pointing to the folder I had open in front of me, she said, "That might be overkill, but maybe there's something in there you can use."

"Thanks," I said. "John Ghent has only eight paintings, mostly mid-nineteenth- and early twentieth-century, European and American."

"Popular stuff. It really depends on whether his paintings fit in with a sale they're putting together. If they do, he might sell them in the next few months. If not, he may have to wait a while. Is he in a hurry?"

"I don't think so. Should I tell him to call the main number for the auction house and say he has some paintings to sell?"

"He could. They're always on the lookout. That's how they make money. You could also call the guy who signed those letters and tell him I referred you. Is it high-end stuff?"

"Not like Tiffany's collection. There are a couple from the Barbizon school. A couple are American Regionalist, but not Grant Wood or Thomas Hart Benton. I don't recognize the signatures. It's all quality stuff, but there's only one that might be worth a lot of money and I have some questions about it." I pulled out my phone and displayed the photo I had taken of the Picasso in the game room of the Ghents' house.

Sandra scowled for a moment and then took my phone so she could look closer. "That's interesting."

"What do you mean?"

"It has some things in common with Tiffany's Picasso," she said.

"I thought so too: the crude sexuality, the odd brushwork, the feeling of ridicule. Also, they both have—I may be crazy about this—a lack of energy. They look like Picassos, but I don't get Picasso's energy from them. There's no spark. I'm sorry I can't give you a better description of what I mean."

"I think that's a fair description."

"You see it too?"

Sandra nodded.

"What do you think it means?"

She thought for a moment. "Didn't Tiffany say something the other day about her painting being done in Picasso's final years?"

"Yes. She mentioned that when we were having coffee after dinner at her house."

"Apparently he wasn't doing his best work then."

"A lot of critics said that about the late paintings when some of them were first exhibited."

Sandra sat back and folded her arms. "Of course, there could be another reason."

I waited for her to explain.

"Maybe he didn't paint them," she said.

"Do you think Picasso had someone working with him in those final years? Perhaps a student or an apprentice made some of the paintings?"

She shook her head. "I wouldn't know about that. I'm saying it's possible someone painted them more recently."

I nodded "They could be forgeries."

"It's possible."

I took a sip of my latte before replying. "It seems like a leap from saying they don't feel like his best work to saying they're fake."

"Maybe not such a leap. Thomas Hoving, the legendary director of the Metropolitan Museum of Art in New York, trained his curators to write down their first impressions of a piece being considered for purchase. They had a detailed process for authenticating an item before purchasing it, but he said those first impressions almost always proved to be true."

I had the feeling that comes when riding down in a fast elevator. Your insides seem to float for a moment. "So, both

Tiffany and Anne Ghent bought Picassos from the Redburn gallery and both might be forgeries."

She nodded.

I could easily have spent two hours with her going over all the implications of what she was saying, but I remembered what had brought me here. "John Ghent has suffered a huge loss this week," I said. "He's grieving the loss of his wife. I hate the thought of dropping this on him. Anne paid over $600,000 for this painting."

"I can understand that," she replied.

"What can I do?"

"Do what he asked. Help him sell the paintings."

"No. I mean, how can I find out if his Picasso is real or fake?"

Sandra had a faint smile as she said, "Before we ask that question, we have to ask why we would we want to find out."

"So I can tell John. Tiffany, too, when I talk to her."

"Tell them what? That they paid a lot of money for worthless paintings? Trust me: They won't thank you for that."

"But then they would know they should return the paintings to the dealer."

"If you tell John Ghent his painting is fake, and he goes to the dealer and says, 'you sold me a forgery,' the dealer might threaten to sue John and you for ruining his reputation."

"I'm not saying he should do that. But dealers will usually take a painting back if a buyer just doesn't like it."

Sandra thought about that for a moment. "How long ago did they buy them?'

"A little over two years."

She shrugged. "I don't know. Depends on the dealer, I guess."

"What is John supposed to do?"

"Sell the painting, if he wants to."

"Knowing it might be a forgery?"

"His wife bought it in good faith from a dealer. It belongs to him now. He can supply a provenance when he sells it. The next buyer can make his decision based on that."

I started to feel angry. "I can't let him do that without telling him Picasso may not have painted it."

"Why not?"

"It's dishonest."

"Did he ask you to authenticate his Picasso?"

"No, but it seems wrong to keep this to myself."

"Unless somebody asks you or John to guarantee the painting's authenticity, there's no reason to bring it up. This is how works of art are bought and sold."

Now I was really teed off. "So, you're saying the whole art market is just people selling fakes to each other."

"Of course not. Most of the time people are buying and selling the real thing. But it happens more than you would imagine. And when it does, everyone keeps quiet about it."

My head was spinning. "Let me get this straight. There could be people out there right now creating forgeries . . ."

Sandra nodded. "They're definitely out there."

"And the dealers are too interested in making a sale to authenticate the works . . ."

"Some of the dealers, some of the time."

"And wealthy buyers don't care so long as they can resell it."

"Typically."

I picked up my cup and found it was empty.

"It's like a high-stakes poker game, and some people cheat," said Sandra. "I'm sorry to dump all this on you."

"Don't apologize."

She pointed to the folder of information on the auction house. "I need to put that back on file at Greenbrae."

"Oh, sure." I handed it to her. "I already wrote down contact info. Thanks."

We walked out onto the sidewalk. The late-afternoon light had only made this spring afternoon more beautiful. We said our goodbyes and walked different directions to our cars.

As I drove back to campus, I thought about Sandra's question: Why do I want to find out if these two Picassos are fake? In my gut I knew I had to find out. That's what art historians do. We answer questions such as, "Who painted this?" If the owners didn't want to know, maybe I could find out without telling them.

As I crossed the steel truss bridge into Blanton, it occurred to me I hadn't talked to Abbie in a couple of weeks. I pulled into a parking space on Maple Street and took out my phone. It was never difficult to find parking in Blanton, a small town that had shrunk when its shoe factory was shuttered many years ago. It survived by providing retail, banking, and legal services to farmers east of Chillicothe, along with a couple of bars and churches and a Chinese restaurant. We who lived on the campus of Cardinal University also depended on it.

"Hey, neighbor," I said when Abbie answered. "Are you back from Pittsburgh?"

"Yep, just got in."

Abbie's partner, Sharon, lived in Pittsburgh and worked for an investment company. Her condo was very nice, as Pat and I had discovered last fall when we drove up and spent a weekend with them.

I heard a sigh before Abbie said, "There's something about leaving Sharon's condo overlooking the rivers and coming back to my little shack in the woods that makes me wonder what I'm doing here."

"The answer is obvious," I said, "you're keeping me company."

"Hmm. How about if we all move to Pittsburgh and keep each other company there?"

"Get me a job in art history, and Pat a job in psychology, and that's a deal."

"I'll keep you posted."

"I'm in Blanton on my way back to campus. Are you in the mood for some Chinese food?"

"That does sound good. Get me some of those walnut prawns."

"Will do. Do you have wine?"

"Now that you mention it, I seem to recall a couple of bottles finding their way into my overnight bag before I left Pittsburgh."

"See you in thirty."

Chapter 12

Since I'd arrived on campus, almost three years ago, Abbie, an assistant professor of economics, had been my best friend and confidante. She had helped me with all kinds of practical matters from hauling furniture from Ikea to learning to drive in snow. Without her I'd have been even slower to grasp the politics of the school. We'd had a lot of laughs together along the way. Since I got together with Pat over a year ago, I'd spent less time with her, but we were still pals, and we called on each other whenever needed.

She wasn't kidding when she called her campus housing a "shack in the woods." We lived on a gravel road called Montgomery Avenue where the college had provided prefabricated plywood housing modules for single faculty. We called them Rabbit Hutches. All faculty started out in them, unless you happened to show up with a spouse and children, in which case you skipped right to a duplex or maybe a detached house. The formula for moving to better housing without enlarging one's household was known only to the Office of Campus Housing.

I parked in front of my Hutch and popped in to change into lighter clothes because the afternoon had gotten warmer than I'd expected. I walked in my front door, looked around the living-dining-kitchen room of my Hutch, and groaned. I hadn't gotten around to cleaning over the weekend and the place needed it.

Fortunately, after living here for three years, I had my cleaning routine down to half an hour. Mostly I had outdoor furniture: a cafe table and two chairs by the back window and two canvas-sling beach chairs by the front window with a little table between them. When I cleaned, I folded all those pieces and stuck them in the bedroom along with the "rug" made of several pieces of artificial turf stitched together. That way I could dust, sweep and mop with only the two tall shelving units to work around.

After reassembling the living-dining-kitchen room, there wasn't much to do in my bedroom since it contained only my futon on a frame and a night stand. My closet and the shower-only bathroom were partitioned off one side of the room.

I promised myself I would clean before I went to bed.

After changing my clothes, I walked fifty yards up the road, carrying the take-out food with me, and knocked.

She opened the door saying, "The sauvignon blanc isn't chilled, so we'll have to get along on beaujolais."

"Works for me."

When I walked into Abbie's Rabbit Hutch, I felt a familiar yearning. She had an oak pedestal table with two oak chairs upholstered in brocade, two armchairs, and a wool rug. Of course, there was a trade-off. Since the living-dining-kitchen room of a Rabbit Hutch was ten feet by fifteen feet, and had a miniature kitchen built into one corner, all her full-size pieces of furniture were touching each other, which made it necessary to side-step around them.

While Abbie opened the wine and poured two glasses, I unpacked the cartons of food and prepared two plates, walnut prawns for her, General Tso's chicken for me.

Once we were seated at her small pedestal table and had each eaten a few bites, Abbie asked, "So, what have you been up to?"

"Last Saturday, Pat and I went to a dinner party at the home of Tiffany and Dale Milman."

Abbie paused with a morsel of food on her fork, halfway to her mouth. "Dale Milman? Why do I know that name?"

"He's some kind of investment guru. Their house looks

like the setting for a movie based on a Jane Austen novel."

"Hedge fund manager," said Abbie. "That's it. Sharon mentioned him."

"Really? His office is in Columbus. Why has she heard about him in Pittsburgh?"

"He made a lot of money very quickly. That tends to get the attention of people in her line of work. So how was the dinner party?"

"I felt like a fish out of water, except for the part where Tiffany showed us her art collection."

"Ooh! I bet that was nice."

"Yes, she certainly has spent some money on her pictures. One in particular is supposed to be by Picasso."

"Supposed to be?"

"I have some questions. I sort of invited myself back Tuesday afternoon so I could ask her about it, and it became clear she's not all that knowledgeable. I think she wanted something spectacular for her collection and paid a dealer for it without thinking about it."

"Was she able to answer your questions?"

"We didn't get that far. When I pointed out to her the painting is sexually explicit, she got upset and left the room."

"Sounds like a wasted trip, unless . . . do you have a scholarly interest in Picasso?"

"No, I haven't done any work on him. I probably wouldn't even be thinking about it except that on Wednesday I heard one of the guests at the dinner party, Anne Ghent, had been murdered. Then on Friday her husband called saying he wants to sell all her paintings, and yesterday I went to look at them and found a Picasso very similar to Tiffany's."

"Whoa! That's a lot of information. How was this woman murdered?"

"She was shot in the parking lot of a mall. The police are treating it as a robbery and they've arrested someone."

"That's terrible. And the husband . . . well, he's not wasting any time."

"I'm not sure how much to read into that. The point is Tiffany and the murdered woman were friends, and both had paintings that are supposed to be by Picasso but seem a little off."

"In what way?"

"They might be forgeries."

"For heaven's sake, Noonan, you do have a way of stumbling into these things. Did you ever consider going into a less stressful career, like—I don't know—hostage negotiator?"

"Very funny."

Abbie cleared our plates and added a drop of wine to her glass. "More for you?"

"No thanks."

We moved to the easy chairs covered in brocade next to her front window. I curled up in one, and Abbie stretched her long legs out in front of the other.

After a sip of wine, she asked, "Are you going to tell Tiffany about her friend's Picasso? Or tell the husband about Tiffany's Picasso? Or tell either of them that something seems fishy?"

"I don't know. I've just come from a meeting with Sandra Carlini, registrar at the Greenbrae Art Museum."

Abbie shrugged. "Never heard of it."

"It's in Elbridge, over toward Dayton. It just opened at the end of last year. She said that, once a fake gets in circulation, it's very difficult to expose it. Whoever owns it doesn't want to see a million-dollar investment become worthless."

"I can understand that."

"So presumably neither Tiffany nor John Ghent would want to know their painting might be fake."

Abbie pursed her lips for a moment. "Or they might want to know so they can unload it before word gets out. It's called the 'greater fool theory of investing.' When you buy stock in a company, for instance, you might not worry about whether the company is profitable so long as you're sure you can always sell that stock to a greater fool than yourself."

A memory from the previous Saturday night flashed before me. I sat forward and put both feet on the floor. "Dale Milman talked about Tiffany's paintings like they were investments. When we first arrived for the dinner party, he asked me something about calculating the returns and the risks. The rest of the evening, Tiffany talked about her collection of paintings as a hobby. She said she wanted to become a connoisseur, but she doesn't know much about art, and I'm not sure how interested she really is. What if Tiffany's art talk is just a smokescreen, and the paintings are really part of Dale's investment portfolio? Is that possible?"

"Sure. I remember reading about a guy who helped start a tech company and made hundreds of millions. He used third parties as buyers, so he could remain anonymous, and built a collection of rare musical instruments, mostly violins and violas. He kept them in a fireproof vault."

"Nobody played them?"

"Nope. To him they were just investments."

"So, these super-rich guys buy these things to make money?"

"Not so much for the return on investment. For that they spread their money around in different kinds of stocks, bonds, real estate, and so on. They diversify so if the market in one area goes down, they have some other investments that hold their value. Things like paintings, musical instruments, vintage cars, and rare wines don't go up and down in price like the stock market does. Investors buy these things just to park some money, usually a small percentage of their wealth."

I took a moment to feel dizzy over the idea that a small percentage of the Milmans' wealth was probably several times the amount of money my family would ever see.

"So, this would not be a big deal for Dale Milman?" I asked.

"What do you mean?"

"If one painting turned out to be worthless, he wouldn't

be all that upset?"

"I wouldn't say that. Guys like him play to win. If you made it known one of his expensive paintings was worthless without first giving him a chance to unload it, I think he would be very upset with you."

I went cold all over, wondering if Anne Ghent had learned something was wrong with the paintings she and Tiffany had bought and had started talking openly about it. I wondered how far Dale Milman would go to stop her.

"I guess I had better tread lightly," I said.

Abbie nodded. "Think real hard about how far into this you want to get."

"I have to go. Thanks for the wine."

"Thanks for the food."

Chapter 13

The morning light was especially flattering to the redbud trees on the hillside below my office window. In the past three days their buds had opened, adding pink and white accents to their spring display. The white blossoms of the dogwoods were at their height. I knew from my two previous springs in the foothills this was about as good as it got.

My thoughts were not nearly as pretty on that Monday before class. I'd had almost forty-eight hours to think about calling Detective Brian Murphy of the Shawville Police Department. I still wasn't sure communicating my suspicions about Curtis Diaz was the right thing to do, but I recalled that slogan, "If you see something, say something," and dialed.

Once I had him on the line, and we'd introduced ourselves, I said, "I'm calling about the murder of Anne Ghent."

"Thank you for calling." He spoke slowly as if he were taking notes. "Do you have information that might be relevant to our investigation?"

"It might be. I attended a dinner party at the home of Tiffany and Dale Milman a week ago, Saturday. After dinner Tiffany invited the women to join her in another room to see her collection of paintings. She also invited Curtis Diaz because he is the director of the Greenbrae Art Museum. Anne Ghent turned to Curtis and said, 'You're just one of the girls.'"

"I see. And did Mr. Diaz appear to be upset by this remark?"

"He didn't say anything, but it was an awkward moment."

"Did Mrs. Ghent and Mr. Diaz exchange any other remarks during the evening?"

"No, but since then I've visited the Greenbrae Art Museum and learned that Curtis is gay and doesn't want to share that in his professional life. He became very upset when his co-worker mentioned it in front of me. So, I thought perhaps he may have had some resentment toward Anne Ghent."

"Understood. But you're not aware of any altercation involving Mrs. Ghent and Mr. Diaz that may have occurred after this dinner party and before the night of the murder?"

"No. I wouldn't know about that."

"Alright. Thank you for calling. We'll be sure to look into this."

"I know you've arrested someone. I just thought you should know someone else may have had a motive."

"Of course. We're always glad to get information from the public. As I said, we'll look into this. Thanks for calling."

We hung up, and I took a moment to rest my eyes on the hillside below my office window. I was fairly sure Murphy's notes would go into a file and be forgotten, if not into a waste basket. I wished I could have made my story more convincing, but it was all I had. I'd done what I could. Maybe others would call in with information that would widen the investigation.

I shook off my doubts and returned to the mystery that most occupied my mind. My conversations with Sandra and Abbie the day before had sharpened my sense of where the hazards lay in pursuing the authenticity of the Picassos, but had not changed my predicament. As a historian I needed to know. Also, I didn't feel good about helping John Ghent sell his Picasso to a "greater fool." And if there were still any chance of developing the Milmans as donors, I had to decide whether I could bring up the problem without making enemies of them.

As I knew from every research paper I ever wrote, when every thought brings you back to a question you can't answer, it's time to ask a different question. I had asked Sandra: How do we find out if the Picassos are fake? What if instead I asked myself how I could find out if they are real?

This reminded me of an idea I'd had when I left John Ghent's house: Call the dealer and ask a few questions about both Picassos, specifically about their provenance. Maybe they were from the same owner. The heirs of that friend might have offered both paintings for sale at the Redburn Gallery.

If that were true, I would know they were probably real Picassos—not very good ones, but real. That would satisfy my scholarly curiosity and relieve me of ethical concerns about helping John Ghent sell the painting Anne bought. Tiffany would still have the problem of owning a painting that was mildly pornographic, but she could solve that by selling it if she wanted to.

I wrote, "Call Redburn Gallery," at the top of my to-do list for the afternoon.

My Modern Art class went well. Most of the students had become familiar with the artists, and all of them could recognize their influences in pop culture, advertising, decoration, and design. This made them more eager to know about the artists and their art. This got me to thinking we should teach art history by starting with the present and working our way back in time. Of course, I couldn't think of a single art history book that was organized that way.

At the end of class I waited by the table at the front of the room to speak to Elaine Wiltman about her paper. Since my conversation with Pat on Friday evening, I had resigned myself to accepting her paper so long as she added an acknowledgement of the article that was its source. I didn't like the idea, but, as Pat had explained, I had no way around it at this point.

When she followed the others to the door, I called out, "Elaine?"

She appeared not to hear me and followed the others

through the doorway.

I stepped into the corridor and called out, "Elaine?"

Her friend, walking next to her, put a hand on Elaine's shoulder and said something to her. Elaine shook her head and walked faster.

I couldn't see why she would want to go on avoiding the issue. She'd had the weekend to get over her panic at finding out her paper was based on a published article, and she had my permission to add a note about the source.

From here on it was up to her. She could either amend her paper and hand it in or ignore it and get no credit for the assignment.

When I got back to my office, I found out why she had ignored me. I had an email from Vera Krupnik, dean of the School of Liberal Arts and Sciences, asking me to meet in her office with the dean of the School of Business on Friday at 11:15 a.m. to discuss Elaine Wiltman's paper. There was no further explanation.

I could not recall an instance in which deans got involved in grading a student's paper. There was a grade appeal process in which the student wrote to the faculty member and the chair, who might forward the appeal to an Academic Policy Committee. But that did not involve deans, let alone the deans of two different schools.

I left my office, walked down the three flights of stairs to the ground floor, and then trotted back up to the third floor just to wake up my brain. There's nothing like an infusion of oxygen to help you think straight.

When I came out of the stairwell, I kept going down the corridor, past my office, and peeked into the office of the chair of the Art Department, my chair, Frank Rossi. He was dressed in a purple blazer with a deep green shirt and an aqua-blue tie—being a landscape painter, the colors were both arresting and complementary. He wore the clothes well on his trim, fifty-ish frame and kept his salt-and-pepper hair trimmed short.

Since he was alone and seemed to be scanning his

computer screen and clicking on things, I assumed he was involved in nothing more serious than web-surfing and knocked.

He waved me in. "Nicole. Good. Sit. What's up?"

"Thank you, Frank. I just got an email from Vera Krupnik asking me to meet with her and the business-school dean on Friday to discuss the grade for a term paper from a student in my Modern Art class."

Frank frowned for a moment. "Grade?"

"When I handed papers back to the class on Friday, I told her she had to acknowledge her source before I could give her a grade. The paper is obviously a paraphrase of an article in *Art Journal*. She said she didn't know what I was talking about and refused to acknowledge the source. I thought by this morning she would have changed her mind, but she refused to talk to me. Then I got this email."

Frank grimaced and shook his head as if he had just smelled something disgusting. "Two deans?"

"I don't understand it either, Frank."

He reached for his desk phone. "Talk to Vera. See what this is about."

"Is that really a good idea?"

He paused.

"What if this wasn't her idea?" I asked. "What if she's accommodating a request from the other dean?"

Frank leaned back to think about that. "Possibly."

"I really just wanted to find out if you knew what this was about or if you had ever heard of such a thing before."

Frank shook his head. "No clue."

"Alright then, I guess I'll go to the meeting and see what they want. The situation is pretty straightforward. I can't imagine what they want to talk about."

Frank nodded. "Keep me posted."

Conversation with Frank was always an exercise in filling in the blanks, yet I always came away feeling that everything that needed to be said had been said. He had stuck by me last year when I accidentally ran afoul of the other painter in the Art Department, Irving Zorn, so I considered myself lucky to have him as my chair. Being in uncharted territory wasn't especially comfortable, but I felt reassured by the idea that there were no expectations for a professor in my situation.

Chapter 14

After my meeting with Frank, I returned to my office and woke up my computer so I could look up contact information for the Redburn Gallery in New York. I made the mistake of glancing at my inbox and found an email from Mira Robillard, the artist to whom I had sent a contract for showing her work in the college's gallery in the fall. The news was not good. Her mother had fallen ill, diagnosed with cancer, and would soon be undergoing chemotherapy. Mira had to put everything on hold and go to Texas for at least six months to care for her. She apologized and hoped she could exhibit with us next year.

I felt awful for Mira. I couldn't imagine how I would feel if one of my parents fell deathly ill, and I didn't want to think about it. I wrote back with condolences, cautious encouragement, and a promise to keep in touch. After that I wrote to the Gallery Advisory Committee, telling them of Mira's situation, and saying I would write to the next artist on our list, with an offer to exhibit in the fall.

Getting back to the item at the top of my to-do list, I went to the website for the Redburn Gallery. It showed them to be dealers in miscellaneous modern and contemporary art. They were located in Chelsea, a neighborhood on the lower west side of Manhattan. Judging by a search for "Chelsea art galleries," so were dozens of others. From their page for staff, I copied the name of the sales director, Lester Jappling.

Before I could call the gallery, a new email appeared in my inbox. Greta Oswald had written, not just to me, but to all members of the Gallery Advisory Committee calling for a meeting to discuss offering an exhibit to the next artist on our list. True to form, she had proposed a meeting time, noon on Wednesday, which would ruin my chance to get a bite to eat and catch my breath before my one o'clock class.

I was not surprised that Greta had ignored my message, in which I said I would write to the next artist on our list. Working with Greta on the committee last year, I had learned her need to meet was powerful, driven by the desire to have some sort of social life. I knew that if I refused, it would cost me a lot of energy. With everything else going on, I didn't have energy to spare. I wrote back to her, Bert, and Shirley, saying I would be happy to meet.

Hoping for better luck than I'd had all morning, I dialed the number of the Redburn Gallery and asked for Lester Jappling. Fortune smiled, and I was put on hold.

Jappling turned out to be one of those people who answered the phone by saying his name but making it sound like a question. "Lester Jappling?" Thus, he confirmed his identity and asked why you wanted to speak with him in only two words.

"Good morning, Mr. Jappling," I replied. "I'm Dr. Nicole Tang Noonan at Cardinal University in Ohio."

"Excuse me, what university?"

"Cardinal. Like the bird."

"I've never heard of it."

I felt like asking him if he'd heard of Heidelberg, Wilberforce, College of Wooster, or any of the dozens of other small colleges in Ohio, but I restrained myself.

"You're not one of those for-profit schools are you?" he asked.

"No. We have a long history, but recently changed our name."

"And why are you calling me?"

I decided then that Mr. Jappling and I were going to get along just fine, whether he liked it or not. Adopting my pleasant phone voice, I said, "I am assisting Mr. John Ghent in the sale of paintings purchased by his late wife."

"Ghent? Anne Ghent? Anne is dead?"

I wondered if he was on a first-name basis with all his clients. "I am sorry to bring you that news, Mr. Jappling. One of her paintings . . ."

"How did she die?"

"I don't know the full story. According to news reports, she was shot when someone tried to rob her."

"Oh, my god!"

"If you would prefer, I could call back another time."

"No. What is it you want?"

"The provenance of a painting she bought from you."

That brought him up short. "I'm sorry. I don't know what painting you're referring to."

Yet he remembered her first name, and, according to the file John had given me, which I had open on my desk, she had bought only one painting from him. "In the fall of last year, she purchased a painting by Picasso, approximately sixty by seventy-six centimeters . . ."

"Of course. What is it you want?"

So, he did remember it. "The provenance."

"The provenance wasn't an issue when she bought it."

"I'm sure it wasn't. Mr. Ghent would like to make sure it's not an issue when he sells it."

"He shouldn't be concerned."

"He wouldn't be concerned if he had the necessary information. From whom did you buy the painting."

"That's confidential."

"You must have informed Anne Ghent when she purchased it."

"The painting came to The Redburn under very special circumstances. A family needed to liquidate certain assets and needed to keep the transaction confidential."

"I understand. People aren't eager to advertise that they're selling off their paintings, but surely to establish ownership they would have had to . . ."

"It wasn't simply a matter of financial need. The family was . . . uh . . . under some duress. I can tell you they received the painting directly from the artist toward the end of his life."

"That's good to know. Do you have letters or any other documentation relating to their transaction?"

"Yes, but I cannot share those with you or Mr. Ghent. As I said, I agreed to keep our business confidential."

"Mr. Jappling, you leave Mr. Ghent in a difficult position."

"I don't agree. It's a marvelous painting. You have only to look at it."

Of course, I had looked at it, and it didn't look very good, but there was no point telling him that. I tried another strategy. "If there is something wrong with the provenance . . ."

"You've no right to say that. If you make that sort of unfounded accusation, there could be legal consequences."

"Then can you tell me if you have sold any other Picassos for this same family?"

"I am happy to reassure you about the provenance of the Ghents' Picasso, and certainly I am sorry for Mr. Ghent's loss, but I am not here to open our sales records to you, certainly not over the phone."

I decided to appeal to his sense of greed. "Perhaps you could tell me if any similar paintings by Picasso are likely to be available in the near future."

"I thought you said Mr. Ghent wanted to sell his painting. Why would he want to know if any others are for sale?"

"I'm consulting with several clients." The lie rolled so easily off my tongue.

"Then tell one of them to buy Ghent's painting."

"That is a possibility, but I want to give my clients as complete a picture of the market as I can."

"I'm sorry I can't help you any further. Good day, professor."

We hung up.

I had to admit I'd had a little fun pushing the guy and

hearing him get flustered. I don't usually enjoy upsetting people, but his tone suggested his lofty perch in the New York art world made him unaccountable to a lowly professor at a university whose name he'd never heard. Also, it became obvious he was covering up something when he remembered Anne but pretended he didn't remember selling her a painting.

By saying the seller's family had received the painting directly from Picasso, he hinted at a good reason for thinking the painting was real, but so long as he withheld the identity of the family, he wasn't really saying anything. Likewise, by refusing to say whether he had sold other paintings owned by the same family, he wasn't helping me to understand how two, inferior, late-period Picassos turned up in the same gallery at the same time. If they weren't being sold by the same family, forgery seemed the next most likely explanation.

I decided to take another stab at convincing myself they were real. After my one-o'clock class, Art Appreciation, I went to the library and used their databases to search for scholarly articles on Picasso published in the past thirty years.

When I had a list of five authors who had published frequently over that period, I scanned their titles to find the ones who had addressed Picasso's development as an artist, in particular his stylistic innovations. I chose Dr. Sidney Rosenberg because he had written about Picasso's late work.

My plan was to send him photos of Tiffany's Picasso and Anne Ghent's Picasso, and ask if he agreed that these two paintings were likely done in the last years of the artist's life.

But first I needed a photo of Tiffany's Picasso.

Chapter 15

The secretary at Fairhaven seated me in the reception room instead of showing me into the drawing room. That spoiled my plan. Last Tuesday I had maybe five minutes alone with the paintings before Tiffany joined me, ample time for snapping a picture of the Picasso. I would have to switch to plan B, as soon as I figured out what it was.

I occupied myself by looking out the French windows to the garden, which was blooming nicely, and by getting reacquainted with the paintings Tiffany had bought when she was buying to please herself: two scenes of the same pond, one at sunrise, the other by moonlight. They probably weren't good investments, though they would hold their value and give pleasure as long as she lived.

After fifteen minutes I heard footsteps coming along the corridor, not from the direction of the dining room and drawing room, but from the opposite end of the house. When Tiffany came around the corner and walked to me with both hands held in front of her, I was startled by her weak smile and washed-out appearance. Perhaps she had slept poorly or caught a virus, but I suspected the shock of her friend's death had shaken her. She wore sneakers, sweatpants, a t-shirt, and hoodie. The fabrics and the tailoring told me her sweats probably cost more than my best clothes, but still it seemed almost humorous to see the lady of such a grand house dressing down.

"Nicole, so good of you to drop by."

As we shared a social hug, I said, "Happy to. Thanks for

agreeing to give me another look at your collection."

"Of course," she said. "What good are they if nobody looks at them? Come on."

As we stepped back, and I looked at her up close, fatigue and grief showed equally on her face.

"I was so sorry to hear about Anne Ghent," I said. "I know you were friends."

She reacted as if seized by cramps. I felt her hands squeezing my shoulders as she struggled to maintain her balance. She sobbed a bit and wiped tears from beneath her eyes. She nodded rather than saying anything.

When she had stabilized, she put an arm around my shoulders and we walked down the corridor to the door of the drawing room. "Thanks for sending me that list of books."

I had to think before recalling the list of titles I had sent after last Tuesday's visit. "Oh, those. Were they helpful?"

"I ordered them," she said. "They haven't come yet."

As we walked to the drawing room, I had a momentary panic over whether that Picasso would still be there. When I last saw her, Tiffany was so upset when I pointed out the explicit depiction of sexual intercourse in the painting, I feared she may have put it somewhere out of sight. However, when we entered the room, it was still above the fireplace, looking stranger than ever.

I chose the sofa that put my back to the fireplace so I wouldn't stay focused on the Picasso. Tiffany sat across the coffee table from me. I let my eyes wander over the paintings on the adjacent wall. There was, as I had recalled, much to admire. "I notice you have two pieces that are not oil paintings," I said. "Are you thinking about starting to collect drawings and watercolors?"

"No. They don't really cost enough, although this one did, because it's by Matisse," she said, pointing to the drawing in pencil of a reclining, nude woman. "And that one did because it's by Chagall."

"Excuse me, do you mean you don't want to buy less

expensive works?"

Tiffany gave out with a sigh that came from deep inside her. "Dale had some money set aside, and he told me to buy some art. I realized that, if I kept buying paintings like the ones in the reception room and dining room, it would take me forever to spend it all, and, by the time I had, we wouldn't have enough wall space in the whole house for them. So, I went to some galleries and auctions and read about the artists who cost more and are supposed to be the best." She scanned the wall next to us without glancing over at the Picasso. "I've still got a ways to go."

I didn't ask how much she had to spend, though I was dying to know.

So, these paintings were not so much a collection as a shopping spree. Abbie was right. Dale Milman was diversifying his portfolio by parking some money in art. Tiffany was his investment broker. Her interest in art was an afterthought.

As I struggled to think of something else to say about the paintings, I remembered I had to come up with plan B for getting her out of the room so I could take a photo of that Picasso. "Excuse me," I said. "I'm feeling a little dehydrated from the drive over here. May I have a glass of water?"

"Of course," said Tiffany. "We can have tea if you like."

"Just water," I said.

She pulled her cell phone from the pocket of her hoodie, tapped on the screen, and put it back in her pocket. "So, if you hear of any good auctions or gallery shows, let me know. I try to keep up with them in the magazines, but half the time I can't understand what they're talking about."

A young woman in a maid's uniform knocked, entered, and approached.

"Water, please," said Tiffany.

The young woman curtsied and departed.

Of course. Why would Tiffany get me a glass of water when she had staff for such things? So much for plan B.

She looked at me and smiled, though her expression didn't have much energy behind it. "Learning about art is harder than I thought it would be. I come from a family of doctors, so we never had a lot of art around the house. Not real art, I mean, just posters and some photos we picked up on vacations. I had an art course in college, and it was good, but we didn't really do that much."

The young woman came back with a tray on which she carried a pitcher of ice water and two glasses. They were so beautiful, I thought they must be Waterford crystal.

After the maid curtsied and left, Tiffany poured each of us a glass. "How about you?" she asked. "Was your family into art?"

"Not so much," I said. "My mom is a librarian. Dad works construction. But I grew up near an art museum. In the summers, when I was out of school, Mom and I would walk over to it and eat in the cafeteria and walk around and look at the paintings and sculptures."

"Really? There was a museum right in your neighborhood?"

"Yes. We live a few blocks from Golden Gate Park, and the museum is in the park."

"Oh, so that's how you got started in art. I didn't follow in my parents' footsteps either, although my brother and sister did. Dad, Tom, and Jen are all doctors. I took an education course in college and liked it, so I became a teacher, but I never taught. I had babies instead."

"How many children do you have?"

"Two. A boy and a girl. Dale junior and Missy."

"They must keep you busy."

"Not so much anymore. They're all grown up now. He's in California and she's in Virginia. When they moved out, I started playing tennis at the club, and I got pretty good at it. I was just getting so I enjoyed playing when my knee blew out. That ended my tennis career. I lost almost two years with the surgery and rehab. It would have taken me another two years to get back to where I was. It just wasn't worth it."

I swallowed hard and breathed deep to shake off the sadness I was feeling from her story.

She sat up straight and seemed to muster all her courage as she said, "So, really, this art thing came along at a good time for me. I was looking for something to do. It's harder than I thought it would be. That's why I'm so glad you're willing to spend some time with me."

I put on a happy face and said, "The last time I was here, you mentioned you have Jansen's art-history book. Why don't we see what it says about Henri Martin?" I gestured toward the pointillist scene of boats in a harbor.

"Oh, is that how you say his name? He's French. Sure. I'd like that."

She pulled out her phone, and for a moment I thought plan C had failed, but she put it back in her pocket and said, "I'll just run to the library and get it myself. Will you excuse me?"

I smiled and nodded, and she left the room.

I waited to hear her footsteps in the corridor before getting up, pulling out my own phone, and walking over to the Picasso. Opening the camera app seemed to take forever, but I got the painting centered in the viewfinder and tapped the button just as the door behind me opened.

I turned and saw the maid frozen in place, watching what I was doing. As soon as I looked at her, she pulled her eyes away from me, fetched the pitcher from the coffee table and departed. No curtsey, this time.

I breathed deep to still my beating heart, sat, and took a long drink of the water left in my glass before tucking my phone back into my purse. I focused my eyes on one of the landscapes and tried to look like someone who was appreciating art, while my mind tried to figure out whether there was any reason for that maid to tell her mistress I had taken a picture of the Picasso. Based on movies about what goes on in stately homes, I guessed servants never mix with their masters or the guests. On the other hand, perhaps there was some code among the servants about protecting the interests of the family.

What was done was done. I could only await the repercussions.

Chapter 16

Tiffany came back carrying the book clasped to her chest with both arms. As she laid it on the coffee table, she asked, "Would he be in the chapter on impressionism?"

"Let's just look up his name in the index," I said.

I came around and sat next to her so we could both look. We read about Martin and compared him to Seurat. We looked at the photos of other great French paintings of the late 1800s. When I told her the gardens Monet painted were still there in Giverny, and open for the public to visit, she said she had to get Dale to take her there.

The maid brought back the pitcher re-filled with ice water. She never even glanced at me.

After half an hour, it seemed Tiffany was tired, so I thanked her and excused myself. I left her sitting back, looking at her paintings with renewed interest.

As I drove back to campus, I thought of the students I had known at Fuchs College, now Cardinal University, over the past three years, and of those I'd encountered as a teaching assistant in graduate school. Some remained uninterested in art, satisfied with a passing grade; others made a game of recognizing styles and guessing the artist's name, which can be fun; a few recognized the age-old struggle of artists to communicate their experience of life in visual symbols and responded with appreciation.

Among all of them, I'd never had a student other than Tiffany who had taken an interest in art because she'd been told to spend millions buying it. This was, I supposed, as good a way as any of getting started.

As the past half hour showed, she was a bright and curious student. Since service to the university was part of my job, and Tiffany was a potential donor, I was indirectly being paid to teach her. But teaching her surely involved telling her if one of her paintings was fake. That made me feel a little better about taking a picture of her Picasso without asking her permission.

When I got home, I emailed my pictures of Tiffany's Picasso and John Ghent's Picasso to Professor Rosenberg, asking if they were consistent with what he knew of Picasso's late work.

Wednesday's meeting of the Gallery Advisory Committee was to be brutal in its efficiency and breathtaking in its brevity if I had anything to say about it. Since the committee had previously approved a list of artists we wanted to exhibit, agreeing on a replacement for Mira Robillard shouldn't have needed much discussion.

As I approached the door of the small seminar room on the second floor of the Arts and Humanities Building, I heard nothing going on. Stepping inside, I found Shirley and Greta sitting in silence, each in her own world of thought. When I dropped my folder on the table and greeted them, they nodded to me and ignored each other.

As I sat, Bert came in the door. Such a well-timed entrance could only have been achieved by lurking in the hallway watching for me to enter first. "Sorry I'm late," he muttered, as he came to the table.

"Let's begin with your report, Shirley," I said. I was glad to see that surprised her. When she looked at me wide-eyed, I explained. "I haven't received an email from you, so I assume no one else has either. Why don't you tell us your thoughts on the gallery's emerging brand and save yourself the trouble of writing to us?"

Her look hardened a few degrees before she replied. "I

thought the purpose of this meeting was to approve a replacement for Mira Robillard, so I have not prepared that report."

I wasn't letting her off the hook that easily. "I recall you felt pretty strongly about the branding issue at our last meeting. Since you're familiar with the other three artists we're considering, surely one of them strikes you as more relevant than the other others to what you perceive our emerging brand to be."

Through clenched teeth, she said, "No."

"Alright then, we'll set aside all discussion of branding and marketing until a later meeting."

Shirley glanced at Bert and sat back in her chair with folded arms. If she was going to use our meeting time to flirt, she'd have to come up with a new angle. I glanced at Bert to see if he recognized the situation, but his eyes were on the papers on the table in front of him.

"The next artist on our list is Hassan Shebib, sculptor." I passed out copies of a page with photos of four of his works. "As you may remember, he works in stainless steel wire, creating dynamic human and animal figures. They look powerful and massive, but are, in fact, lightweight. This would be our first sculpture exhibit. I think this could get a lot of attention from the campus community and in the area."

"How big are these?" asked Greta. "How many could we fit in the gallery?"

"That's a good question," I said, even though the dimensions were noted on the sheet. "These are all table-top size, so we'll have to install some pedestals. I think we can borrow from other programs on campus."

Greta gave a guttural groan. "That's so complicated and it sounds expensive."

"Every exhibit has its challenges, Greta," I said. "I'm sure it can all be worked out."

"I'm just thinking of you," she said. "This gallery demands so much of you. I don't know where you find the time."

"No need to worry. I enjoy it. It supports my teaching."

Greta seemed not to have heard me when she said, "I vote we should keep it simple."

There was no way of knowing whether she meant that as an alternative to the sculpture exhibit or as a general statement of policy. "At the moment, Greta, there is nothing to vote on. Your concerns about the sculpture exhibit are duly noted. Does anyone else have any thoughts about exhibiting the work of Hassan Shebib?"

Bert kept his eyes on the page of photos I had passed out. He seemed determined not to look up until the meeting was over and it was time to leave the room.

Shirley startled me by speaking in a loud voice. "I agree with Greta. This is much too ambitious. Stainless steel sculptures must weigh tons. Who is going to handle them? Will we have to hire a crew of movers? Do we have the budget?"

"As I said, Shirley, they are in fact lightweight. As you can see in these photos, they are made of stainless steel wire that outlines the subject. Weight will not be an issue."

Shirley shivered as she said, "We haven't had time to think about this. I'd like to do some research. I move we postpone this decision."

I turned to Bert who was still studying those four photos. "Bert, what are your thoughts on exhibiting the work of this artist?"

Without looking up, he said, "Interesting work. This sheet gives dimensions but not weight."

"That's because weight is not an issue," I said. "Some of these are less than a foot tall. The largest is eighteen inches high and less than two feet long. They are made of bent wire. They are mostly air."

"Still it wouldn't be difficult to find out," said Bert. "Just ask the artist."

"Obviously we don't have enough information," said

Shirley. "I move we adjourn until Nicole can give us a report from the artist."

"Seconded," said Greta.

"Fine," I said, startling myself. It came out louder than I intended. "I will report to the committee by email, and, if—as I suspect—weight will not be a problem, I will go ahead with sending a contract to this artist."

"That might be premature," said Shirley. "Perhaps we should meet to discuss this when we have all the information."

"Absolutely," said Greta.

Bert glanced at his watch. "I need to leave the meeting early. My department is getting together and I have to be there. I'm sorry." He slipped the papers on Habib into his portfolio.

"I think we're done here," said Greta.

"Unless Nicole has something else for us to discuss," said Shirley, staring at me with arms folded.

"That's all for today," I said. "Thanks for coming."

I fiddled with my papers and file folders while they left the room and made sure to hear their footsteps fade away before getting up and walking back to my office on the third floor.

I had called Shirley's bluff by insisting she give us her thoughts on the gallery's brand, and it had become apparent she had none. I had taken away her strategy for flirting with Bert during the meetings, but this was a strategic error. She retaliated by siding with Greta against me.

Worse, Bert seemed to be sulking all through the meeting, and he did not back me up when it came to contacting the next artist. I couldn't imagine why his attitude toward me and the committee had changed. When we met at the coffee bar on the previous Friday, he thanked me for intervening when Shirley flirted with him at the last meeting. Had he changed his mind about that? That seemed unlikely.

I made a note to call him before sending out my next email to the committee. I wanted to get us back on the same page.

In the meantime, I would find out the weight of Habib's sculptures, though I felt silly about asking such a question. What difference could it make whether they weighed ten ounces or two pounds? Nonetheless I would inform the committee and would seriously consider going ahead without having another meeting.

All through my class and office hours Thursday morning, I felt a strange mixture of excitement and anxiety. It started when I got a text from Pat saying he couldn't go with me to the memorial service for Anne Ghent because he was behind on a research deadline and needed to work through the afternoon. I assumed he also wanted to spend some time in the weight room. He didn't have a rigid schedule for his workouts, but, when he needed one, everything else could wait.

If we'd shown up at the service as a couple, it would have been obvious we were following a social convention—we'd met the Ghents at a dinner party almost two weeks ago and were paying our respects and supporting the grieving husband—but I felt awkward about showing up on my own and wondered if I should apologize for Pat's absence when I talked to John and the others or just let them make their own assumptions.

While trying to calm myself by nibbling on a PB&J and flipping through emails, I saw a reply from Dr. Sidney Rosenberg to my question about the authenticity of Tiffany and Anne's Picassos. He began by saying, "What you ask is impossible," partly because Picasso produced so many paintings in his last years. He ended by saying, "No critic or historian would attempt to give a valid opinion based on pictures taken with a cell phone."

Guys like him really annoyed me. He could have just said he couldn't tell by looking at the photos. He didn't have to imply that I was stupid for asking.

I shut down my computer, tidied up my office, and loaded my backpack before heading back to my Rabbit Hutch so I could get in my car and make the ninety-minute drive to Shawville, where the service was being held at two o'clock. While doing so, I considered the possibility that my project to authenticate both Picassos was now dead in the water.

As I walked down Ohio Avenue and turned on to Montgomery, a new possibility occurred to me. I might see Sandra Carlini at the memorial service. As registrar of Greenbrae, she surely knew how Greenbrae authenticated paintings when they were added to the museum's collection. I might call upon her.

Since John Ghent had given me access to Anne's paintings, she might be willing to look at Anne's Picasso. If she saw no reason to call in a curator, I would feel more confident about advising him to sell it, and would be relieved of any duty to tell Tiffany her painting might be questionable.

After changing into my most somber dress clothes, black dress and black blazer, I hit the road with a renewed sense of purpose.

Chapter 17

The funeral home sat beside a four-lane road on the outskirts of Shawville. Though I got there a few minutes after two, there were only a dozen cars in the parking lot. The thought of walking in and introducing myself to a handful of strangers gave me the chills.

Instead of turning into the driveway, I went past and drove through a wooded section before coming to a shopping plaza with a coffee shop. I went in and got a small cup of tea.

Twenty minutes later, I drove back, saw more cars in the lot, parked, and went in.

After signing the guestbook, I looked into the parlor to the left of the foyer and saw perhaps twenty people, clustered in small groups. John Ghent was not among them. Perhaps there was a separate parlor for family members. The only person I recognized was Sandra Carlini. Lucky for me, she was sitting by herself on a loveseat in the corner. I joined her.

"I thought I might see you here," she said.

"It seemed like the thing to do, even though I met Anne and John so recently. You must have known them for a while."

"A little over a year," she replied. "But whenever I saw them it was at events like that dinner party—social, but with a professional undertone. Let's face it, people like us are always going to be visitors to this social circle."

Looking across the room, I noticed Curtis Diaz talking to a couple in the corner. "Curtis is here too."

Sandra suppressed a smile. "Curtis made it clear we both

would be on hand to remind everyone that there's a worthy cultural institution just down the road."

"Really?"

"He wasn't that blunt about it, and he won't be obvious about it here, but he knows what he's doing: reminding people with money that we're part of their world."

I turned so I could talk to her directly. "I've been thinking a lot about our conversation at the coffee shop the other day."

She nodded. "I hope I didn't throw too much information at you."

"Not at all. You gave me a lot to think about. You helped me understand why the marketplace makes it so hard to expose forgeries. Now I have another question for you: What happens when one of these fakes gets donated to your museum? Do you ever worry about that?"

"I have nightmares about it, and so does every curator and registrar."

"So, wouldn't it be worth trying to take these fakes out of circulation whenever you can?"

"We can't police the art market. You've seen what it's like at Greenbrae. We're juggling chainsaws just to keep the place open. And it's not much different at big museums."

"But you have a process that makes certain you don't put a fake in your collection, right?"

"Most of the time."

I waited a moment for that to sink in. "Are you saying some of these fakes end up hanging on a wall in a museum?"

"Yes."

"But that must be rare."

Sandra grimaced. "There's a lot of disagreement among museum people about how common this is. Let's just say it happens more often than most people think."

For a moment I thought I was going to hyperventilate. "As an art historian, this is really starting to upset me. If people see these forgeries in a museum and think, 'That's what a Picasso looks like,' the forger changes our understanding of

Picasso's work."

"That's what we're all worried about."

I had to restore my sense of reality by staring out the window for a few seconds. When I felt like I was back on earth, I turned back to Sandra. "What about all this technology? X-rays, carbon dating . . ."

"And spectographic analysis, isotope dating, ultraviolet, infrared—yes, all these techniques and more have been applied to authenticating paintings."

"Then why can't you put a painting through these tests and prove whether it is real or not?"

"Commercial labs charge a lot of money. Let's say a museum pays one of them to test a painting. If the lab proves the painting is fake, the owner of the painting can dispute the findings and sue for damages. Introducing technology does not change the fact that there's always someone who does not want the fake detected. For a lot of museums, usually it's not worth the expense."

I thought about what she was saying for a moment before asking, "Would you look at a painting for me?"

She looked surprised. "Which one?"

"The other day I showed you a photo of a Picasso Anne Ghent owned. You noticed it was similar to Tiffany's, and that's what made you say they could be forgeries."

"I was just thinking out loud."

"I understand, but John wants me to help him sell it, and I don't feel right about doing that if there's a good chance it might be fake. Plus, I need to know whether I'm looking at the real thing. I am a historian after all."

Sandra held her breath for a moment before saying, "I don't mind helping you, but you must understand a couple of things. First, I'm not a curator. I'm not trained to authenticate, but I've worked with curators, and I'm familiar with a lot of their tests, so I could give you a general idea. Also, you must never tell anyone I gave you an opinion on the painting or that Greenbrae had anything to do with this. Curtis is right: That's not the business we're in."

"Understood. I won't tell John or anyone else you even looked at it."

"Also, you'll have to bring the painting to Greenbrae. Obviously, we can't keep this confidential if I go to Ghent's house to look at it."

"I see what you mean. I'm not sure how I can arrange that, but I'll get back to you."

"Okay. We'll pick a time when Curtis won't be around."

"I appreciate it."

She shrugged. "It's an interesting problem, even if it's not relevant to Greenbrae."

The room had become more crowded, and people were starting to move into the chapel through the double doors at the far end of the parlor.

Sandra stood up. "Excuse me. I'd better hit the ladies' room before the service begins."

My insides buzzed with excitement over the prospect of having the Ghents' Picasso examined, but first I had to convince John to let me take his painting out of his house. I could tell him the provenance from Redburn was sketchy, which was true; therefore, an independent assessment would help to convince a buyer to pay top dollar for it, which was probably also true. But, he would want to know who was doing the assessment. I would have to think of a reason why I couldn't tell him that.

Of course, I couldn't talk business with him at his wife's memorial service. I might have to get back to him next week. That would give me time to think through the details.

Few people were left in the foyer, so I stood and walked toward the chapel.

Dale Milman stepped in front of me. "I heard you're helping John," he said.

"I'm here to give some moral support like everyone else."

"I mean with the paintings, the ones Anne bought. I understand he's selling them."

The man had no shame. "If you have questions about them, you should talk to John."

"I just want to know why he called you in."

"I'm not comfortable discussing that with you or anyone other than John."

He folded his arms across his chest. "Here's the deal: Anne recommended Redburn Gallery. That's why Tiffany went there to buy the Picasso we have. So, when I hear John has called in an expert instead of going back to Redburn to sell his painting, it sounds to me like there could be a problem."

I glanced around hoping to see someone coming our way to interrupt this conversation. Unfortunately, people seemed to be steering away instead.

"First of all," I said, "I'm not an expert on Picasso. Second, John's concerns are much simpler than yours seem to be. But, as I said, you should talk to John about that."

I started to walk around him, but he side-stepped in front of me.

"What I want to know is, are they legit?" he demanded.

Fortunately, a couple of people had glanced our way, aware of Dale's confrontational tone.

"I really can't tell you anything," I said.

"If there's a problem, I want to know," he snarled.

This time, when I tried to go around him, he let me get past.

Dale had just proven what Abbie told me about "guys like him." They play to win. Clearly, he didn't mind making a scene at a memorial service to protect his assets, including the "extra" few million he was "parking" in the art market.

But would he kill someone who threatened those assets? He might have thought Anne Ghent was a threat.

This was the second time in a week I found myself wondering if Dale had a motive for murdering Anne. I couldn't do anything about it, but I knew someone who could. Detective Brian Murphy would be hearing from me ASAP.

Chapter 18

I walked up the center aisle of the chapel and saw John had sat in the front pew on the left, along with a few people his age and several people around my age. I guessed the younger ones must be his children along with their spouses, though I'd never heard Anne or him speak of children.

The several rows behind him were mostly filled. I took an aisle seat halfway back so I could watch which way John went after the service and catch up with him to offer condolences.

The organist had begun to play softly while I was thinking about my situation, and more of the pews had filled up. I sensed movement on my right, turned, and saw that Maria and Ernst Becker had come up the side aisle and were making their way into the pew where I sat. Recalling my conversations with them at the dinner party from hell, I wasn't eager to chat with either of them. The service was about to start, and that, I hoped, would put an end to conversation.

Maria sat beside me and said, "Some funerals are sadder than others."

Not knowing what to make of that, I nodded in her direction and looked past her to acknowledge Ernst's arrival. He sat looking to the front of the room, seemingly unaware of anyone around him. The expression on his face suggested something monstrous weighed on his mind.

I kept my eyes focused on the front of the room as Maria swiveled her head to look past me to the other side of the aisle. "I thought there would be more people here," she said. "Looks like mostly extended family and older friends. I don't see many people from the club."

Fearing she would keep talking until she got a response, I said, "I wouldn't know. I only met them at the Milmans' dinner party."

My strategy didn't work. After a minute she said, "Is this a busy time of year at your university?"

I turned to face her, said, "Perhaps we can talk about this after the service," and turned back to the front of the room without waiting for a response.

That won me a few moments of silence, which allowed me to hear sobbing from the aisle behind me. I didn't want to gawk, but I glanced to my left and saw Tiffany walking by with her arms folded and a handkerchief held over the lower half of her face. Dale walked a step or two behind her, his eyes scanning the pews on both sides.

"I don't know what she's so broken up about," said Maria. "She hasn't had a good word to say about Anne since she wrecked her knee playing in that doubles tournament. Everybody says she blamed Anne for pressuring her into it, and I guess that's true, but really it was up to her to know her own limitations."

"You'll have to excuse me," I said, without looking in Maria's direction. Carrying my hat and my jacket, I walked down the aisle, left the chapel, and found the ladies room. I combed my hair, just to give myself time to calm down, and thought about happier times so my face would lose the expression of disgust I felt over Maria's malicious gossip.

I thought about going home but decided to stay for John's sake.

Returning to the chapel, I chose a seat several rows further back and sat behind a tall man to make it difficult for Maria to see me even if she turned all the way round to look for me.

The funeral director began, "We are gathered here this morning to celebrate the life of Anne Ghent and to comfort those she leaves behind." He read a meditation suggesting our lives on earth are part of some larger cosmic pattern, after which he introduced a friend of the Ghent family, who spoke about Anne's childhood in Indiana, high school accomplishments, college career, and life with John. The funeral director then introduced a soprano, who sang, "You are the Wind Beneath My Wings," a favorite of Anne's. The director closed the service by inviting us to meet with the Ghents in the family reception room. The organist played, and the Ghents walked down the center aisle.

I followed the instinct of herd animals for avoiding a predator. I waited until a good number of people were walking down the aisle and walked among them. It worked. I made it out of there without Maria Becker catching up to me.

In the foyer, most people went directly out the front door of the funeral home. I followed the few who turned up the corridor toward the family reception room. There I found a dozen people, scattered in twos and threes, and at the far end John Ghent sat on a sofa speaking with people on the chairs facing him.

As I edged my way toward John, I heard someone call my name, looked to my left, and saw Curtis Diaz smiling and gesturing for me to join him and the couple he was standing with. "Nicole, I'd like you to meet some people." Turning to them, he said, "This is Dr. Nicole Noonan of Cardinal University. She's been consulting with us at Greenbrae, and we're hoping she'll help us jump-start our education program, which is central to our mission."

He told me the names of this couple and their interests, but I lost track of all that because I was trying to think what I would say if they asked me about my "consulting" with Greenbrae, since I didn't know what Curtis was talking about. Fortunately, they were more interested in themselves, and I had only to continue smiling and nodding until I could excuse myself to go and offer my condolences to John Ghent and his family.

I understood Curtis was trying to enhance the prestige of

Greenbrae Museum by suggesting it had ties to universities in the area, but I didn't appreciate being put on the spot that way. For a moment, I thought how bizarre it would be if he had killed Anne because she threatened his fundraising efforts by outing him at the Milmans' dinner party and was now using her memorial service to raise funds.

I hovered near the end of the room until one of the people in the chairs facing the sofa got up. While John turned aside to speak to someone next to him on the couch, I took a seat. When he turned back and saw me, he smiled, reached out a hand, and said, "Nicole, thank you for coming."

His cheeks were pink and his eyes were bright. Apparently, he'd already had his "orange juice." "You're welcome," I said. "I'm sorry for your loss."

He took a moment to absorb that before saying, "Thank you." He gave my hand a squeeze and let go.

I was about to ask if I might call him in a few days when he asked, "Any ideas so far about selling the paintings?"

I hadn't wanted to get into that, but I couldn't ignore his question. "Yes, although there's one thing we should talk further about. Shall I call you this weekend?"

"What is the issue?"

"I called the Redburn Gallery about the Picasso and spoke to the man Anne dealt with. He wasn't able to tell me much about the painting's provenance. Without knowing that, it may be hard to sell it for the best price. So, I've spoken to someone who's willing to look over the painting and tell me if there are any questions a potential buyer would ask about its authenticity."

"Is this person some sort of expert? Someone who works for a gallery or an auction house?"

"My contact has asked me to keep this confidential, since they're doing this assessment as a favor."

John thought for a moment before saying, "That makes sense. Thank you for setting this up."

"I'm happy to do it. One further concern: I will need to

borrow the painting and take it to them."

John waved that concern aside. "That's no problem. Whatever you think is best."

"I'll call you this weekend to set up a time."

He frowned. "It may have to get done this weekend. I'm thinking of going away next week to stay with my daughter's family for a while."

"Alright, then. I'll call you tomorrow."

"I can't thank you enough."

"Don't mention it. Again, I'm sorry for your loss."

My chest started to feel tight. I now had a deadline for getting that painting authenticated.

I looked for Sandra as I left the reception room but didn't see her. She wasn't in the front parlor either. Before getting in my car, I sent her a text: "Call me when you get a chance."

As I drove back to campus, my thoughts were jumbled. I was willing to pick up the painting, take it to Greenbrae, and return it the same day, but, if Sandra wasn't available during the coming weekend, all that would have to wait until whenever John came back from staying with his daughter. If he didn't mind postponing, there was no reason I should, but I didn't like the idea. Since the status of his painting was tied up with the status of Tiffany's, I wanted to get this resolved.

My phone rang, and I managed to pull it out of my purse and tap the answer button and the speaker button without running my car into a ditch.

"What's up, Nicole?" asked Sandra.

"I'm on the road, but I see a gas station coming. Hold on."

Though it wasn't unusual to see people holding phones to their ears while at the wheel, I didn't want to try it. Having started driving less than three years ago, I didn't have a lot of confidence. I turned into the driveway of the station, and went to a parking space for the mini-market.

"Hi Sandra. Thanks for getting back to me so soon."

"No problem."

"I just left the memorial chapel. When I talked to John Ghent, he asked about selling the paintings, so I told him it would be worthwhile to have the Picasso examined. I never mentioned you or Greenbrae."

"Thank you."

"He has agreed to let me take it from his house for that purpose, but he says it has to be this weekend, because he might go away next week. Does that work for you?"

"Hang on a sec." After a few seconds, she said, "Okay. I'm free, but I'm trying to pick a time when Curtis won't be around. He's supposed to attend a meeting and luncheon on Saturday. It's in Cincinnati, and he's going there directly. I don't imagine he could get back to the museum before about two p.m. Could you meet me at Greenbrae with the painting around eleven? That way we'll be done in plenty of time."

My deadline just got closer. "No problem," I said. "I'll give you a call Saturday morning to let you know when I'm on my way."

We hung up and I sat in my car waiting for the prickly feeling in my stomach to go away. I couldn't leave campus on Friday before about two fifteen. That meant I would have to ask John to let me pick up the painting at his house late in the afternoon, or early on Saturday morning.

It then struck me I would be transporting a painting that might be worth nearly a million dollars. I had seen painters bring their work to the gallery on campus covered in bubble wrap and boxed, though their paintings were priced in four or five figures rather than six.

The mapping app on my phone gave me directions to a packing and shipping store not too far out of my way back to campus.

I stopped into the mini-market for a coffee-in-a-bottle and hit the road.

Chapter 19

On Friday morning I received John Ghent's email saying I could pick up his Picasso at ten o'clock, Saturday morning. That fit with Sandra's suggestion that I get to Greenbrae by eleven, so I confirmed with her.

Since I still had forty-five minutes before class, I called Detective Murphy.

"Good morning, Detective. Nicole Noonan, Cardinal University. I called you on Monday about the murder of Anne Ghent and the possible involvement of Curtis Diaz."

"Yes. I recall our conversation. I can't tell you anything further about that. We don't discuss ongoing investigations."

"I understand. I'm calling about another person who may be involved."

After a few seconds he said, "We're always happy for any information we receive from members of the public. Go ahead."

He didn't sound happy. "Yesterday I attended a memorial service for Anne Ghent. It was at a funeral home. There were perhaps a hundred people there."

"Yes. I'm aware of that," said Murphy. "I was there."

"You were? I didn't see any police officers."

"I was in plain clothes. Do you have some information for me?"

"Yes. Before the service started, I was talking to someone in the foyer, and, when I got up to go into the chapel, Dale Milman confronted me, demanding to know about some consulting I am doing for John Ghent. He was very aggressive."

"I think I remember this. He was speaking to an Asian woman, and, from where I stood, it did not seem like a pleasant conversation."

"That was me. So, you know about this?"

"I couldn't hear what either of you were saying."

"John asked me to advise him on selling some paintings Anne bought. Dale wanted to know what I'd found out about them because his wife, Tiffany, bought a painting from the same gallery that sold Anne one. Of course, I wouldn't discuss John's business with him."

"And he wouldn't take no for an answer. Is there anything else?"

"Yes. Talking to Tiffany, I've come to understand Dale has invested a lot of money in their paintings and is very concerned about anything that might affect their value."

"That's understandable."

"But it's more than that. He's a wealthy man. He takes his investments very seriously. If he suspected Anne Ghent knew something about the value of one of his paintings, he would not have hesitated to confront her as he did me. Things could have escalated, and he might have killed her."

"Alright, Dr. Noonan. I think I have the overall picture. Thank you for calling in."

"I hope you understand, I'm just saying he had a motive."

"Of course. That's perfectly clear. We'll follow up. Thank you."

He hung up.

Hearing myself saying all that to him, it sounded much less convincing than it had when I discussed it with Abbie or when I replayed it in my own head. I couldn't blame him for cutting our call short. At least I had put the idea into his head.

And it was interesting that he had attended the memorial service. If he were completely satisfied that Tyrell Johnson was the murderer, he wouldn't have bothered. Perhaps my previous phone call about Curtis Diaz got him interested in people from the Ghents' social circle.

With that resolved, I settled in to have a normal day as a college professor, so much so that I almost forgot my meeting with Dean Vera Krupnik, scheduled for eleven fifteen. I saw it on my calendar when I returned from my morning class, dropped what I was doing and dashed to her office on the second floor.

When I arrived with a minute to spare, the dean of the School of Business, Oscar Bayliss, was already in conversation with the liberal arts dean. He was a big, boney man around 60 years of age with only a fringe of white hair left on his head and he kept that clipped close. He wore a well-cut, tan suit and a white shirt and brown, striped tie, and sat with his legs crossed and one elbow propped on the arm of his chair.

Whenever I saw Vera, she made me think of a bird. She had a long thin nose and small eyes. She wore her short hair teased up on top and used lots of makeup. She wasn't much taller than me but was more substantial, and she emphasized that by wearing bulky tweeds.

Both greeted me cordially. I still couldn't imagine why two deans wanted to discuss grading a student's paper with me. When I remembered that the chairman of the Art Department, Frank Rossi, had never heard of such a meeting, I began to feel butterflies in my stomach.

Dean Krupnik began by saying, "Thank you for taking time to meet with us this morning, Dr. Noonan. We're here for an informal discussion of the problem with Elaine Wiltman's paper for your class, Modern Art. Why don't you give us your view of the situation?"

That suggested the deans were already aware of someone else's view. I thought about asking what that might be, but decided not to be confrontational. After all, I had nothing to hide.

"She turned in her term paper," I said. "I discovered it had many similarities to a published article on the subject, and asked her to document her source, either within the text or in an endnote."

"And did she do so?" asked Krupnik.

"No. She denied using a source."

Dean Bayliss uncrossed his legs, leaned forward and asked, "Dr. Noonan, did you at any time make clear what the consequences would be for the student if she followed your instructions and documented her source?"

"I made clear that the purpose of my instruction was to teach her how to acknowledge a source, as scholars must do. I told her once she did so, I would give her paper a grade."

Bayliss maintained his poker face as he asked, "And did you tell the student how she could be penalized for failing to acknowledge her source?"

"There was never any question of penalty. I made clear she had to complete the assignment to get a grade."

I looked to Dean Krupnik, hoping for an explanation of why the dean of the business school was asking about consequences and penalties, but her face was as blank as his.

Bayliss forged ahead with his questions. "Dr. Noonan, does your syllabus include a definition of the word 'plagiarism?'"

"No."

"How much time did you spend in class at the beginning of the semester discussing plagiarism and the proper handling of sources?"

"None, and I'm not aware that it's standard practice at this university. Modern Art is an upper-level course, so this can't be the first time these students have heard about acknowledging sources. But why are we talking about plagiarism? That wasn't an issue with Elaine's paper."

Instead of answering me, Bayliss looked to Dean Krupnik, who said to me, "Again, Dr. Noonan, this is just an informal discussion of the situation. We just wanted to hear from you, so we are fully informed."

"Why? What's going on?"

As if she hadn't heard me, Krupnik looked to Bayliss,

who nodded. Turning back to me, she said, "I think we'd like to talk this over. If there are any further concerns, we'll be in touch. In the meantime, thank you for coming in."

No one said a word as I stood up and left the office.

I went directly downstairs, out the front door of the Arts and Humanities Building, and walked out College Avenue past the chapel, toward the athletic fields. There are fewer buildings out that way, and therefore fewer people to run into. I needed silence so the meeting I'd just left could echo in my mind without interruption. None of it made any sense.

When I got to Fellbach Circle, I turned off and went to Pat's house.

Chapter 20

After knocking at Pat's front door, I let myself in. The aromas reaching my nose told me he was making lunch. My spirits lifted.

"Want a grilled-cheese sandwich?" he asked, as I walked into the kitchen.

"I'd love one," I said, taking a seat at the table.

"You look like you've seen a ghost."

"I'm not sure what I just saw."

"Where were you?"

"Dean Krupnik's office."

"What did she want?"

"The business-school dean was there too."

"What did they want?"

"Do you remember last week I told you about the student in my Modern Art class who turned in a paper based on a published article and said she didn't use any source?"

"Right, and my guess was that someone wrote it for her, and she didn't know that person was paraphrasing an article. Whatever happened with that?"

"She has avoided talking to me and I haven't given her a grade. Then I got this email to meet with the deans, and today Bayliss hit me with all these questions about plagiarism. Who said anything about plagiarism?"

Pat walked over to the table with a grilled-cheese sandwich on a plate and put it in front of me. "I'll take a shot at that question," he said.

He walked back to the counter by the stove and started

making one for himself. "Maybe your student went to the person who wrote the paper for her and complained that the paper was copied from an article. The person who wrote the paper said, 'Just tell her you forgot to add the footnote.' Maybe someone's roommate overheard all this and said, 'That's plagiarism! They can kick you out of school for that.'

"So, your student called her parents and said, 'My art professor is accusing me of plagiarism,' without mentioning, of course, she had someone write the paper for her. Then the parents called the dean and complained that some incompetent art professor is threatening to ruin their daughter's career before it even gets started, and, if that happens, they'll sue the university. So, the dean has to convince himself that you didn't handle things properly so he can justify letting the student off the hook."

"How can he let the student off the hook? The paper is for my class."

Pat shook his head. "You've got me there."

I was too stunned to take another bite of my sandwich. "How do you know this kind of thing goes on?"

"I don't, really. I was just trying to imagine who might have said something about plagiarism. I guess that's easier to do that when it's not my problem."

"So why is the dean of the business school involved?"

"Maybe Elaine's major is in the School of Business."

"So where does that leave me?"

"As they say on the news broadcasts, 'awaiting further developments.'"

Pat sat down with his sandwich and we ate in silence for a few minutes.

"Busy this weekend?" he asked.

"Tomorrow I am. It has to do with that painting that belongs to John Ghent. I'll be done by mid-afternoon. I'll tell you about it tomorrow when I'm here for our night."

"Fair enough. Or we could ban work-related conversations and instead talk about where we're going to hang out this summer."

Last summer, when Pat and I had been together about five months, we visited his hometown, Rochester, Minnesota, and my hometown, San Francisco, California. This would have been an unimaginable luxury on an assistant professor's salary, but I had a standing offer from Mom and Dad to pay my airfare any time I wanted to come home. In this instance, they also paid Pat's airfare because they were so excited that I had a boyfriend with serious potential. They seemed to think it was important for me to form a lasting relationship by the time I reached thirty.

"What did you have in mind?" I asked.

"How long do you think your parents would have us?"

Last summer, Mom and Dad let us stay in the studio apartment behind the garage on the ground floor of their attached house in the Inner Sunset neighborhood. Almost all the houses on the west side of town have such an apartment. They're called "in-law suites."

"Let's think about that," I said. "Whenever I call home, Mom asks about you, and how your classes are going, and if you have any new recipes for her to try."

"Your mom is really sweet."

"Yes, she is. I have to remind her that I also have classes that are going well, and sometimes I come up with new recipes too."

"I'm sure she's just being polite."

"Also, the last time I was on the phone with them, Dad wanted to know if you had watched that game when the Giants beat the Reds, and also 'What does Pat think about the Reds' new left-hander?'"

"Your dad's a great guy."

"Yes, he is. So, based on our phone calls, I'd say Mom and Dad would have us for as long as we want to stay."

"Okay then," said Pat. "We'll spend the summer in San Francisco."

"Not the whole summer. We have to visit your family

too."

Pat frowned. "I'll stop by for a few days on the way back to campus."

"No. I want to spend some time with your mom and your sister."

"Okay. We'll both stop by, but, really, we don't have to spend a lot of time there."

"Why not? I liked Rochester. I thought it was interesting." I'd never been to the Midwest except to attend the annual College Art Association convention when it met in Chicago.

Pat winced. "Farm country."

"Rochester is not exactly a farm town. It has the Mayo Clinic. And I enjoyed the Rochester Art Center. Small museums have some amazing exhibitions. And Minneapolis is only ninety minutes away."

"Well, we don't have to decide right now."

"Alright, Mr. Gillespie, you're off the hook for tonight, but don't think we're skipping Minnesota."

I got to John Ghent's house a little after ten on Saturday morning. It felt great to be out of the dress slacks and blazers I wore all week at school and to move around in my overalls with a long sleeve t-shirt underneath.

The neighborhood looked as uninhabited as the last time I'd visited. When I came to the door with my big, flat box and roll of bubble wrap, he answered the door almost immediately. As before, he wore a white dress shirt with no tie, wool pin-striped trousers and loafers.

"Good morning, professor," he said with a smile on his face. "Come on in."

As I came into the foyer, he held up his tall glass of "orange juice," wiggled it so the ice cubes rattled, and asked, "Can I get you something?"

"No thanks," I said. "I'll just pick up the painting and go. I don't want to be late for my appointment,"

"What time do you have to be there?"

"Eleven."

"Do you have far to go?"

"I'd rather not say. As you recall, I have to keep this confidential, so I think it would be best not to hint about where I am going."

He snickered. "Oh, sure. I get it. Hush, hush! Alright, then, right this way!"

He waved toward the corridor that led to the room with the paintings and I walked ahead of him. I had come prepared to comfort the grieving husband, but I could see that was unnecessary. He was again taking his comfort in liquid form.

The library had chairs for reading and a small writing desk, but no large surface for me to work on. I started by unrolling a piece of bubble-wrap twice as long as the painting and spreading it out on the floor. After covering it with a piece of tissue paper, I took the painting off the wall, and lay it face down on the wrapping. On my hands and knees, I pulled the rest of the sheet of bubble wrap over the back of the painting and began taping it in place.

John, leaning in the doorway and sipping his drink, said, "You're very slender."

Without looking up, I said, "I suppose so."

"I guess that's typical of Asian women."

I felt a cold shiver down my spine. I was vulnerable on all fours, but, if I stood up, I couldn't get on with the job, and it would look like I was open to conversation. I sat back in a kneeling position.

"I don't think this tape is going to be strong enough for sealing up the box," I said, holding up the little roll I was using, "Do you have some package-sealing tape?"

He took a sip and said, "I just might."

He went down the hall, and I could hear him rummaging in his study. I worked as fast as I could and had the picture wrapped by the time he came back.

I pulled the box in front of me and lowered the picture into it as he walked toward me.

"Need some help?" he asked.

"Nope. It fits just fine."

"You hold it, and I'll tape it."

"That's okay," I said, taking the roll of tape from him. "I can manage."

With a few deft moves, I had the box sealed. I set the roll of tape on a chair and leaned the box toward him. "Why don't you carry this out to my car?"

While he picked up the box, I grabbed the remainder of the bubble-wrap and slipped the handles of my tote bag onto my shoulder, being careful to keep it closed so he couldn't see the roll of duct tape I'd brought with me.

I preceded him down the corridor and out the front door. I had my car open by the time he got there. "Slide it right in there," I said, pointing to the floor in front of the rear seat.

Once he had it stowed, I stepped toward the driver's seat and pulled the door toward me. "I should be back between one and two. I'll call if I get held up anywhere."

"Okay," he said. "Thanks for doing all this. It means a lot to me. I can't wait to talk to you about . . ."

I didn't hear the rest of whatever he had to say. I shut my door and concentrated on backing out of his driveway without hitting his mailbox. As I drove through the neighborhood, I kept one eye on the speedometer so I wouldn't put the pedal to the metal, which was what I felt like doing.

By the time I reached the highway I was quivering with rage. I was doing this guy a favor and he was hitting on me. I thought about trying to stop somewhere, get out of the car, and burn off some of my energy, but I was afraid I would hurt myself if I started kicking a tree.

I considered going into a shop for a nice long cup of coffee and hoping the painting was gone when I came back out. "I'm sorry, John," I imagined myself saying to him. "I only ran in for a minute to use the restroom. Too bad about your painting."

I also considered driving my car off a cliff—if I could

find a cliff in this part of Ohio—so I could say to him. "Everything went up in flames. It's a shame about the painting. By the way you owe me a new car."

So, what would I really do? I was having this painting examined partly to satisfy myself and partly to get some information that might be valuable to Tiffany. Since Sandra was standing by at Greenbrae to help me, I resolved to carry through with the plan, return the painting, and give Ghent a brief report. Beyond that I would deal with him by email.

Chapter 21

The parking lot alongside the Greenbrae Art Museum was nearly full when I arrived, so I drove past the front of the building, hoping Sandra might recognize my car. Sure enough, she came out the front door wearing a lemon-yellow sweater with dressy slacks and shoes and walked down the steps to meet me.

"Good morning," she said, and pointed back to the way I had come. "Go through the lot and take that gravel drive around to the back of the building. I'll meet you there." She went back in the front door.

The drive ended in a patch of gravel big enough for a few cars. I got out and looked at the house, recalling which windows belonged to the offices on the second floor and which belonged to the kitchen on the first floor.

As I stood there, the cover on the bulkhead opened and Sandra came up the stairs from the cellar. "Let's bring it in this way," she said.

I slid the big, flat box out of the car and carried it down the stairs.

The cellar was roomy and well lit, apparently having been designed as a working space for the staff of the big house. Sandra led me to a work table in the middle of a large room. The wall nearby had hand tools on a pegboard with storage bins lined up beneath.

After pulling the painting from the box and taking her time unwrapping it, Sandra set it on a table-top easel. I sat in a swivel chair off to one side.

Dark Picasso

"I put some questions out on a registrar's forum," she said. "I wanted to see if anyone had seen any late-period Picassos. I thought if anyone had we could exchange pictures and compare notes. So far nothing has come up, but I'll keep looking."

"Maybe that's good news."

"How so?" she asked.

"If some forger were specializing in late Picassos, it seems like they would turn up more often."

"Or it could be the forger is targeting private owners, and they haven't come to the attention of people working at museums yet."

Thinking about art forgery started to feel like looking down a deep well. "All the same, thanks for checking," I said.

She opened a drawer in the work table, got a scratch pad and pencil, sat on a high stool, and looked at the painting. Every ten or fifteen seconds she jotted something on the pad and then went back to looking.

After doing this for a few minutes, she set her pad and pencil on the work table.

"Do you see anything interesting?" I asked.

"I was just jotting down my impressions. It's a way to make the examination more focused."

Placing her hands on the table, she leaned forward until her nose was less than an inch from the surface of the painting and held it there several seconds.

My curiosity got the better or me. "What are you doing now?"

"Checking to see if the paint is dry."

I laughed. "Seriously?"

She smiled and nodded. "Paint can be dry to the touch and still give off a scent of thinner for years, depending on what conditions it's kept in. Forgers learn to heat a painting in an oven for several hours to burn off all the fumes. This one passes that test. If it is a fake, this forger wasn't a complete beginner."

After looking at the painting for another minute, she took a pad of sticky notes from the drawer in the table, peeled one off, and stuck it to the edge of the table. Then she lifted the painting off the easel, turned it around so the unpainted surface of the canvas was facing her, and steadied it with one hand. With her other hand, she slipped the sticky note between the canvas and the wooden stretcher on the bottom of the painting, and slid it back and forth.

When she pulled out the sticky note and showed it to me, I said, "Looks like dust and lint."

She smiled. "That's what it is. Either this has been hanging on a wall for decades, or the forger was smart enough to put dust and lint under the stretcher so it looks as if it has."

So far all we knew was the painting either was real or was made to seem real. "So far, so good," I said.

"I wish there were a single test that could prove a painting either is or isn't real, but there's no such thing. We just keep trying more tests to see if it fails one or more of them. If it passes them all, it's either real, or it's a very good forgery."

"That's not very reassuring."

"Welcome to my world."

She asked me to take the easel off the work table, and, when the surface was clear, she laid the painting flat, face-up.

"This part may get boring," she said. She switched on a lamp with a big magnifying lens on a crane neck and pulled it into position so it hovered over the upper left corner of the painting. She stared through the lens for a few seconds before moving the lamp to the right a few inches and again staring through the lens.

"What are you looking for?" I asked.

"Broken lines. Variations in color. Anything that doesn't quite line up."

"And what if you find those things?"

"It could mean the forger struggled in spots to make it look like Picasso, or it could mean the painting was damaged and imperfectly repaired at some point."

"So, again, not conclusive."

"That's true, although If I don't find any oddities, that's one less thing to be suspicious about."

I watched for a while and felt frustrated because I couldn't look through the magnifying lens with her. When it was clear she would need another ten minutes to complete her inspection, I took a walk around the basement and saw that Greenbrae still had lots of Horace Oaks' bric-a-brac in storage. There were bronze statues of Greco-Roman heroes, three-quarters life-size; marble cherubs; gaudy chandeliers; and paintings in bubble-wrap.

I wondered if it were wise to store these things in a basement, but the air did not smell damp, and maybe, since the house was at the top of a hill, there was no danger of flooding in a hard rain. It was also likely they couldn't afford off-site storage.

When Sharon pulled the work light away from the painting, I went back over to see what she would try next. "Anything look suspicious?"

She shook her head. "Nothing so far."

She went to the storage bins under the pegboard and got out a hand-held utility light with a long electrical cord attached. After plugging it in, she waved it back and forth over a section of the painting, starting again in the upper-left corner. The hand-held light cast a strange glow over the painting, causing all the colors to change. "Let's see if the UV light will turn up anything."

"Are you looking for anything specifically?" I asked.

"Anything that shouldn't be there," she replied.

"Maybe we'll see the ghost of an image that's been painted over," I said, knowing artists sometimes do that because they're too poor to buy new canvases and forgers sometimes do that to reuse materials from the period they are forging.

"Picasso was rich at the end of his life, so I doubt he'd have done that. Also, I'm looking for anything that shouldn't be there that might have been left behind by somebody working fast. Lots of things fluoresce: fibers, minerals, chemicals. If I see it under UV but not under white light, I'm suspicious."

I watched as she worked over the canvas but saw nothing. Apparently she didn't either, because she switched it off and set it aside without saying anything.

After looking at the painting for another minute, Sandra said, "Remind me: What do you know about the provenance?"

"Not much. The sales director at the Redburn Gallery would say only that this Picasso was sold by a family who had received it directly from Picasso in the early 1970s and that he agreed to keep all the other details confidential. The family doesn't want it known they're selling the painting."

Sharon nodded. "That happens. Maybe they need the cash and don't want to let the world know they're strapped. On the other hand, that kind of story is very convenient for a forger, because the buyer has only the gallery's word it."

"So, we don't know any more than when we started."

"We know one thing. If it is a forgery, it was done by an experienced professional."

I was ready to wrap the painting up, but Sharon was still staring at it.

"Let me check something else," she said.

She lifted the painting off the work table, turned it so the unpainted surface was once again facing her, and brought her nose to within an inch of the canvas. She sniffed a couple of other spots before turning to me with a peculiar smile on her face. "Smell that," she said.

I tried a few spots and said, "I don't smell anything."

"I don't either."

"So, what does that mean?"

"This painting is almost fifty years old. What are the chances it spent those fifty years in a smoke-free environment?"

I shrugged.

"Remember, it belonged to a family. It was probably in a private home. People used to smoke everywhere. It's possible it belonged to two or three generations of non-smokers, but I wouldn't bet on it."

"So, you think it's a fake?"

"I wouldn't say that, but I'm less convinced it's real."

"Well, what should I tell John Ghent?"

"I won't give you an opinion on that because, as Curtis likes to remind me, that's not our business. But if I were at a museum that displayed modern paintings, and a curator were interested in buying this for the collection, I would advise him to hold off until he had more information."

I pulled out my phone and pulled up the photo I had of Tiffany's Picasso. "Here's some more information. Tiffany also bought her Picasso from the Redburn Gallery shortly after Anne bought hers."

"Does hers have the same provenance as Anne's?"

"I asked him and he wouldn't say."

Sandra smiled a little wider. "Now I'm suspicious."

"Why?"

"I would have to examine the other one to see if it's in the same condition. It's possible a non-smoking family got two paintings from Picasso and recently decided to sell them both, but it's also possible that gallery is working with a forger and putting them out one at a time."

"Which do you think it is?" I asked

"I don't know, but I would want more info before paying for a Picasso."

"So, can I tell John Ghent that a potential buyer will probably come to the same conclusion?"

"Sounds reasonable."

While we were packing up the painting, we heard the door at the top stairs of the open.

Chapter 22

From the kitchen above, we heard Curtis call out, "Sandra?"

She looked at me and winced.

The painting was on the work table, almost ready to go in the box. There was no way to get it out of sight.

Curtis came around the corner, looked at me, looked at Sandra, looked at the painting, and scowled.

"Nicole brought a painting over for me to look at," said Sandra.

Curtis glared at her.

"It's John Ghent's Picasso," I said. "He doesn't know I brought it here or that Sandra looked at it. I told him I would have an expert look at it, but that it had to be confidential. He won't know Greenbrae is involved."

Curtis gave no sign of having heard me. When he spoke, his voice had a metallic sound, as if he were straining to control himself. "Sandra, apparently we have a misunderstanding, though I have made myself clear on several occasions. Please come to my office when you're done here." He turned and walked back upstairs.

His words gave me a chill.

"He must have left his luncheon early," said Sandra.

"How much trouble are you in?" I asked.

She waved her hand to silence me. "Don't worry about it. We'll have a talk. I'll reassure him. By next week it will be forgotten."

We finished packing the painting, and she helped me get

it in my car.

As I drove back toward Elbridge, I wondered what Curtis had in store for Sandra. I hoped she was right about how he would handle the situation and how she could handle him. The first time I visited the museum, I wondered if he might have murdered Anne Ghent. Now I wondered whether he would turn violent toward Sandra because she went against his wishes. That seemed crazy, but no one ever said murderers are sane.

I thought about calling Detective Brian Murphy and reporting this latest show of hostility by Curtis. But if my fear was justified, if Curtis lost control with Sandra, a call to Detective Murphy would be too little, too late. I pulled over to the curb, fished my phone out of my purse, and called her.

"Hi, Nicole. Did you forget something?"

I relaxed and exhaled. "I thought I might have left my sunglasses on your work table."

"I can run downstairs and look."

"Don't bother. Next time you're down there, if you see them, set them aside for me."

"Will do."

"Did you talk to Curtis/"

"Yes. He apologized. Once he thought about what you said, he saw the museum wasn't compromised."

"Well, that's good. Thanks again for helping me with John's painting."

We hung up and I drove into town.

On one side of the courthouse square I found Bella's kitchen, offering coffee, sandwiches, desserts, and Wi-Fi—everything I needed at that moment. I parked across the street and took the boxed painting with me into the cafe.

The interior of Bella's continued the lavender and yellow theme on her hand-painted outdoor sign. She must have hired a local painter to decorate the window frames with flowering vines. The tables and chairs were mismatched, old-fashioned wooden pieces, painted to match the decor. I hoped the food was prepared with similar care. I ordered vegetable soup and a lemonade, got the Wi-Fi password, and took a table by the window.

As I sipped the lemonade and let my eyes wander over the street scene, I dreaded having to spend time with John Ghent at his house. The best solution I could think of involved my guy, Pat Gillespie. I decided to call in a batch of IOUs. I phoned him, thinking I would leave a voicemail and hope he called me back before I finished my lunch, but I got lucky. He answered.

"How would you feel about dropping whatever you're doing and meeting me in Elbridge?" I asked. "It's over toward Dayton, along I-71."

"Hmmm." He sounded intrigued. "What's in it for me?"

Using my low, sexy, phone voice, I said, "I can't discuss that right now, but, trust me: You'll like it."

"Is this a lunch date?"

"Lunch can be eaten at Bella's Kitchen on Main street, but there's a little more to it than that."

"How long will this take?"

"We'll be back to your place in time for dinner and our night. And, don't worry, I'll make it worth your while."

"You'd better. I'm skipping my workout for this. I'm on my way."

Knowing Pat would be with me soon made me feel better. I took some time to enjoy my vegetable soup before thinking about what I wanted to tell John Ghent.

The soup was quite good, a little too peppery, but it had a nice mix of vegetables, and they were fresh. When I finished it, I got some coffee, opened my laptop, and set to work planning the next phase of my campaign to prove the Picassos were real.

I'd found most of what I needed when I saw Pat's green jeep roll down the street, slow down as it came to my little yellow car, and go on to a parking space near the corner.

Within a minute, he was striding up the street, eyes scanning store fronts until he found Bella's. In his khaki windbreaker, jeans, and sneakers, he was a good-looking man. He smiled when he saw me sitting by the window. I never got tired of looking at those green eyes.

He went straight to the counter and got himself a latte and a muffin. By the time he sat opposite me, I had finished my online research and closed my laptop.

"I already had lunch," he said, "but these muffins looked really good."

"Thanks for joining me."

He smiled. "I'm sure I won't regret it. What brings you over this way?"

"I picked up a painting from John Ghent's house and took it to the Greenbrae Art Museum so Sandra Carlini could look at it."

"Why did you want me to meet you here?"

"I need you to go with me to John Ghent's house when I return the painting."

"Where does he live?"

"Shawville. It's about fifteen minutes north of here."

"Why do you want me along?"

"When I was there earlier today picking up the painting, he made a sleazy remark to me."

For just a second the gentle man I loved had the look of a killer. "He hit on you?"

"I wouldn't call it that. I think he just thought it would be fun to flirt. I'm sure he'd had more than one glass of his fortified orange juice."

"That's no excuse. I'll be glad to tell him he was out of line."

"I just want you to come with me. You don't have to do anything. Just by being there you'll keep him on his good behavior."

Pat stared out the window for a moment. When he turned back to me he looked more sad than angry. "Alright. I won't say anything."

I squeezed his hand. "It's fine to be the strong, silent type, but don't overdo it. Really. Just be yourself."

"I'm sorry we're still living in a world where a professional woman needs to bring along backup so she can do her job."

"I'm glad you're my backup."

He squeezed my hand. "So, I guess we'll both drive. I'll follow you."

"Before we go, there's something else I want to ask you about. The first time I went to Ghent's house to look at Anne's paintings, I saw a Picasso that has a lot in common with the Picasso in Tiffany's drawing room. They ridicule their subjects. They're crudely sexual and full of cartoonish gestures. It's possible he painted them toward the end of his life, but it's also possible they're forgeries. The art historian in me wants to know which it is, and I feel an obligation to warn John that it could blow up in his face if he tries to sell it."

Pat frowned. "Even though he hit on you."

I sighed. "Yeah. I still have to do my job. Also, if they're fakes, I want to talk to Tiffany about it. I've sort of adopted her as an art student. And, as you know, I'm developing donors."

Pat sat back and folded his arms over his chest. "Alright, so what did you want to ask me about?"

"Will you go to New York with me tomorrow?"

His face went slack for a moment. "Why do you want to go to New York?"

"To talk to the sales director of the gallery where both Anne and Tiffany bought their Picassos. I want to ask him where he got them and how he knows they're authentic."

"I thought you said Sandra was examining Ghent's painting."

"She performed various tests and now she's suspicious of it. She suggested getting the provenance."

"Can't you just call the guy at the gallery?"

"I already did. He got arrogant and blew me off."

"Why would it be any different if you go there and talk to him?"

"If I'm there in person, he can't hang up on me. Plus, I'll have you with me."

Pat glanced at his cup as if he were thinking about getting another latte. "Are you really proposing that we spring for airline tickets to go up to New York and back in one day so you can help some millionaire who made creepy remarks to you?"

"No. While we're at his house, I'll suggest he pay our way. I checked prices," I said, tapping my laptop. "The cost is nothing compared to the price of the painting if it's real. He should be willing to pay so he can feel confident about selling."

Pat's brow was furrowed. He seemed to be struggling to find some other objection.

"Look at it as a free trip to New York," I said. "Maybe we can squeeze in dinner at a nice restaurant before we come back, all paid for by John Ghent, of course."

Pat sighed and shook his head. "My life was not nearly this exciting before you came along, Nicole Noonan. I wonder how long I can stand it."

"I'm eager to find out."

After we left Bella's, I called John Ghent to let him know I'd be there soon to return his painting. I didn't say anything about Pat coming with me.

Chapter 23

I parked in Ghent's driveway, as I had that morning. Pat parked by the curb and helped me get the boxed painting out of my car.

"Quiet neighborhood," said Pat. "On a Saturday afternoon, I would think kids would be riding bikes or kicking a soccer ball around."

"I'm sure they're driven to athletic facilities for those activities," I said.

Ghent answered the door wearing his booziest smile. That smile fell from his face when he saw Pat standing behind me.

"I have some information for you, John," I said. "Where would you like Pat to put the painting?"

I enjoyed watching him struggle to come up with replies. "Here, I guess," he said, pointing to the wall of the foyer.

Pat carried the box in, set it on the floor, and leaned it against the wall.

"My consultant has some concerns about your Picasso," I said. "One of the tests raised questions about its authenticity. We think those questions would best be answered by getting further details of the painting's provenance."

With a scowl on his face, Ghent asked, "Where would you get these details?"

"From the sales director at the Redburn Gallery."

"I thought you took the painting to this expert of yours because the man at the gallery wouldn't give you details. Now you're saying you are going to get details from the gallery?"

"That's right."

The doorbell rang. Pat and I stood aside so John could answer the door.

A uniformed private security guard stood on the doorstep. "Good afternoon, Mr. Ghent. Do you know anything about this car parked in front of your house?"

Ghent looked past the guard at Pat's jeep. "No, I don't, officer."

"That's my car," said Pat. "Is there a problem?"

"I'll have to ask you to move it," said the officer. "Local ordinances don't allow for parking at the curb."

Ghent stepped back from the doorway, glanced at me with a faint smile on his face, and said to Pat, "That's right. We don't allow street parking. You'll have to move it."

"Where am I supposed to move it to?" asked Pat.

Ghent's look of amusement had hardened into a smirk. He shrugged.

Pat looked confused for a moment. When he glanced at me, I knew he was thinking what I was thinking: I was not going to be left alone with Ghent.

I glanced out to the driveway, where my car was parked. "If I move my car forward, I think you can fit your car in behind it," I said. "Let's do that."

Without waiting for a reply, I walked out to my car.

By the time I had started my car, Pat was walking down the drive to his. I moved my car up and waited for him to pull his into the driveway.

As he got out of his car, and came toward me, he asked, "What kind of a town doesn't allow street parking?"

"The kind that likes to harass outsiders," I replied.

The security guard walked by and said, "Thank you, sir. Ma'am, you have a nice day."

We went back to the house and found John waiting for us, still in the foyer. "You were saying something about getting details from the gallery, professor?"

"That's right," I said.

"Why would they give you details now when they

wouldn't before?"

"Because we're going to New York tomorrow to talk to the sales director in person."

Ghent stared at me, glanced at Pat, and turned back to me before saying, "Do whatever you want."

"We'll fly up tomorrow morning and return in the evening. I will send you receipts so you can reimburse me."

A little louder than necessary, he said, "Excuse me! I am not financing your romantic getaway to New York."

"We won't be there long enough to get romantic," I said. "The purpose of this trip is to settle any questions about your painting's authenticity."

"Why would I pay for both of you to go?"

"I don't know my way around New York, and Pat does." I wasn't sure that was true, but it made for a better argument. I trusted Pat would keep a straight face. "It would be easy for someone to harass me." I enjoyed seeing Ghent twitch when I said that. "So, I'd like to have some backup."

Ghent had begun to shift his weight from one leg to the other. "I don't know, professor. This is all getting complicated. Perhaps I should just wait a while before doing anything with those paintings."

"It's your choice, of course," I said. "I'll be away this summer, spending some time with my family in California. So, if you want me to follow up, it will have to wait until the fall. Of course, September is always busy, getting the school year started. Let's say October."

Ghent folded his arms and pursed his lips. Clearly his resolve was weakening.

"John," I said, "if it's authentic, this painting could sell for anywhere from half-a-million to a million dollars, many times the cost of this trip. But, if you sell it for a large amount, and it's later found to be fake, you could find yourself in a tricky position, legally speaking." I wasn't sure that was true, but it sounded plausible.

For a moment I thought Ghent might walk away and

leave us standing in his foyer, but he looked at me and said, "Alright, but I want this settled. Bring me a signed letter attesting the authenticity of this painting, and I'll reimburse you."

"Obviously I can't agree to that. I'm not sure it is authentic."

"You have to promise me something."

"I'll bring you a letter, signed by the sales director, stating what he knows about the painting with details that can be independently verified."

Ghent seemed to mentally review what I'd said before replying, "Agreed. Bring me that letter and I'll reimburse your expenses."

As Pat and I walked down the driveway to our cars, he asked, "Did you ever think about going to law school so you could negotiate trade agreements, divorce settlements . . . things like that?"

"Sure, I thought about it, but art history seemed so much more lucrative."

That made him laugh.

When we got to my car, he asked, "Are you sure you can get this guy at the gallery to write that letter?"

I glanced back at Ghent's house. "I'm not sure of anything right now, but let's not stand around here and talk about it. I'll meet you back at your place."

Once I was on Route 35, I settled in for the cruise back to Chillicothe and started to absorb what had happened. I felt excited about getting to the bottom of an art-history question, but also nervous about the financial part of my agreement with Ghent. I would have to check the balance on my credit card account before buying these airline tickets and hope the cost of them wouldn't go over my limit.

Beyond that were the logistics of getting from the airport—probably Newark—into the city and taking a subway or cab to the gallery's address in Chelsea. I needed some time with my laptop to figure all that out, and it was already late-afternoon.

Perhaps I would give Pat the task of calling the Redburn Gallery, making sure that snooty sales director, Lester Jappling, would be there tomorrow, and making an appointment for mid-afternoon. If I called, Jappling might recognize my voice and refuse to see me.

The largest problem I faced was how to deliver on the promise I had made to John Ghent, a promise I had to keep if I was to be reimbursed. Somehow, I had to get Jappling to give me details—not just a vague description—of the painting's provenance, and put them in writing.

What leverage did I have? Sandra had made clear that nobody ever makes a fuss over forgeries. Instead they prefer to keep quiet and sell to "a greater fool," as Abbie put it. So, if I told Jappling that John Ghent was threatening to sue him, he probably wouldn't believe it.

Sandra had also made clear that galleries are sensitive about their reputations. I could imply that together Ghent and the Milmans could steer people away from the Redburn, but that might not be much of a threat. The Redburn probably didn't have many customers from Ohio.

Perhaps I should be thinking of a carrot rather than a stick. I'd already mentioned "other clients" on the phone with Jappling. I could hint I knew of some buyers who, if only they were sure the Redburn was trustworthy, would flock to the gallery and buy paintings. I could say that writing a good letter of provenance for John Ghent would be just the thing to reassure them. Clearly this was one of life's occasional situations in which a harmless lie is the best tactic.

Chapter 24

I brought my professional outfit—shoes with heels, pants and blazer, all in black, with a white blouse—to Pat's house Saturday evening, and we left at dawn on Sunday. That gave us time to drive to Columbus, get through security, and board our ten o'clock flight to New York.

After landing, we took the Newark Airport Express to Penn Station, where we stopped for slices of pizza. From there we took a taxi to the gallery in Chelsea. We could have taken a subway downtown, but John Ghent was paying.

Everything went like clockwork, and we arrived in Chelsea in time for a walk before our two-thirty appointment with Lester Jappling. The area featured a delightful mix of older, five-story, brick houses and recent apartment buildings made up of whimsical shapes and covered with glass. In the mild spring weather, people sat eating at sidewalk tables in front of neighborhood restaurants. We even went up the stairs from the sidewalk and walked several blocks on The High Line, a former elevated rail line, turned into a garden and walking path.

"I think I could live here," said Pat.

"I could too, although I hear it can be brutal in winter."

"We'd spend winter at our place in Palm Springs."

"All right then, it's settled. When do we move?"

"As soon as we publish our books and royalties start rolling in."

"Do university presses pay royalties?

"I'm planning to write best sellers."

"Oh, good! We can move next summer."

I didn't know why we indulged in these fantasies about things we could never afford, but I doubted we were the only ones who did.

Making our way to the Redburn, I noticed many of the galleries on the streets between Tenth and Eleventh avenues were closed. I had thought the Redburn's website listed hours on Sunday afternoon, but I began to wonder if I'd misread. "Are you sure you made the appointment for today?" I asked Pat.

"Yes," he said. "Jappling read it back to me: two thirty, Sunday afternoon."

We found the Redburn Gallery open. It occupied the commercial space on the street level of one of the older buildings. The big front windows let in plenty of light. The cast-iron radiators and large, old-fashioned woodwork had been painted flat white to blend with the walls.

We browsed the watercolors hanging in the main section of the gallery near the front windows before starting to explore the alcoves further back.

A young woman, dressed as severely as I was, approached to offer assistance. Pat gave his name and mentioned his appointment. She said she would be with us in a moment and went to her desk to make a call.

We walked into another alcove, and I stopped dead in my tracks at the sight of a painting apparently by Picasso. It showed a woman lying nude with emphasis on her lady parts and a man sitting by her with a guitar. The artist had done his best to make them ugly. It was a parody of a lyrical erotic interlude. Like Tiffany and Anne's paintings this one lacked energy, which made it just as unconvincing as theirs.

Pat must have noticed I seemed paralyzed. "Are you alright?" he asked.

"They're multiplying," I said.

The woman rejoined us and said Mr. Jappling would see us now. We followed her upstairs and along a corridor. She knocked on a door and showed us into an office, which was sparsely furnished and loaded with magazines and paperwork.

"Good afternoon, Mr. Gillespie," said Jappling as Pat walked in.

Jappling was half a head taller than Pat and was one of the skinniest men I'd ever seen. His pants were tapered, which made his legs seem longer and thinner. His shirt was partly unbuttoned, revealing a hairless chest. He wore an oversized gray sport coat with the sleeves pushed up to the middle of his forearms. The thick black frames of his glasses contrasted with his pale complexion. He had used some hair product in an attempt to make his sparse blonde hair seem thicker.

When he turned to me and offered his hand, I took it and said, "Professor Nicole Tang Noonan, Cardinal University."

Jappling's face clouded up. "We've spoken recently, haven't we?"

Pat closed the office door.

"Yes. I called you about the provenance of a painting by Picasso you sold to Anne Ghent."

Jappling drew back and looked past me to Pat, who stood patiently by the door behind me.

"My client, Mr. Ghent, needs further details of the provenance," I said.

Jappling glanced from Pat to me and back to Pat. "You're here under false pretenses."

"Not entirely," said Pat. "I am interested in those watercolors, but we have other business to settle first."

"Perhaps we should sit down so we can discuss this," I said.

"We most certainly will not sit down," said Jappling. "We're not discussing anything. You will leave my office."

"Mr. Jappling," I said, "I must inform you that Mr. Ghent's painting cannot be authenticated by the experts who have examined it." Under the circumstances I thought it best to refer to Sandra as more than one expert.

"There is absolutely no need for authentication," said

Jappling. "I have already explained to you: The provenance is perfectly straightforward."

"Then you won't mind if we examine the painting in the alcove downstairs." I glanced over my shoulder at Pat and said, "You did bring the black light with you, didn't you?"

He hesitated for a moment, and I was afraid I would have to wink to let him know I was up to something, but he worked it out on his own. With a solemn look on his face, he patted the flight bag that hung from his shoulder.

"You will do no such thing," said Jappling, stepping toward me. Because of his extraordinary height I had no choice but to tip my head back since I didn't want to give him the satisfaction of seeing me back up. He put his hands on my shoulders and said, "This has gone far enough."

Before I knew what was happening, Pat stepped between us, thrust his hands under Jappling's arms, lifted him off his feet, and pressed him to the wall behind his desk.

Jappling made useless attempts to pull Pat's hands away. After he let out one loud "Hey!" Pat flexed his whole upper body and Jappling was suddenly out of breath. Jappling's jaw moved but he made only a raspy sound. "Uh kuh . . . uh kuh . . ."

I thought he might be trying to say, "I can't breathe," and called out to Pat to stop.

Ignoring me, Pat said, "You should apologize to her."

"Sor—" gasped Jappling.

Pat relaxed his arms and shoulders slightly, and Jappling said, "Sorry."

"Not to me. To her," said Pat.

Jappling looked at me and said, "I'm sorry."

"For what?" asked Pat.

"For pu— . . . for putting my hands on you."

"And are you willing to sit down now and discuss this business in a civilized manner?"

"Yes," said Jappling. "Let's . . . sit down."

Pat released him, and Jappling braced himself against the

wall as he caught his breath and regained his balance. Pat backed up a couple of steps.

Jappling sat behind his desk and reached for the phone.

"Making a phone call right now would be rude," said Pat.

Jappling leaned back in his chair.

I sat opposite Jappling and noticed his hands were shaking. I myself felt uneasy about the way Pat had used force, but decided this was the moment to push ahead.

"Mr. Jappling," I said, "Mr. Ghent needs some information he can verify independently regarding the provenance of the painting his wife, Anne Ghent, purchased from you. You said a family placed the painting with you for sale."

"There was no family, no provenance," said Jappling.

I took a moment to make sure I had heard him correctly. "Are you now saying that what you told Anne Ghent was not true?"

Jappling shook his head. "I'm saying that what I told you was not true. I never told Anne Ghent anything about a painting supposedly by Picasso, because I never sold her one."

This sounded like a lame attempt to lie his way out of the situation. "Mr. Jappling, I know you did. I've seen the painting, and I've seen a receipt for its purchase from the Redburn gallery with your signature on it."

"Yes, I signed that receipt," he said, "but I never sold her a painting."

I studied his face for any sign that he was lying. He seemed to be telling the truth. "Why would you give her a receipt if you didn't sell her a painting?"

Chapter 25

Jappling leaned back in his chair, took a deep breath, and composed himself before speaking. "About two years ago, Anne Ghent came to me and said she wanted to buy a painting by Picasso. I said I would try to find one on the market and broker a deal, and I quoted her a price range. She said she didn't want to pay hundreds of thousands of dollars for a painting, even one by Picasso. I referred her to legitimate online vendors who offer reproductions in the style of Picasso as well as hand-painted copies of paintings by many other artists. The prices are very reasonable and the copies are convincing even to knowledgeable collectors."

"And is that what she did?" I asked.

Jappling hesitated. "I'm not sure. When I mentioned that legitimate vendors do not sign Picasso or anyone else's name to the copies, she said that would not suit her because she wanted a signed Picasso on her wall to impress her friends. I told her I could not help her, but I gave her the names of several art restorers and told her one of them might agree to add a signature to a reproduction. In reality, I knew no one I recommended would do that. I said it just to get her out of my office."

I took out my phone, pulled up the photo I had taken of Anne Ghent's Picasso, and showed it to Jappling. "Where did she get this painting?"

He glanced at it and gave a sour look. "I really don't know," he said. "Maybe she found someone to add a signature to a legitimate copy or maybe she paid someone to make a forgery."

"How would a woman with very little connection to the art world find a forger for hire?"

"Obviously they don't advertise, but art restorers have the necessary skills, and there is a history of restorers making forgeries. Perhaps she kept asking for referrals until she found one."

"I see. Then how did she get a receipt from the Redburn Gallery for a painting by Picasso?"

Jappling's face twisted and he clasped his hands in front of him on the desk. "She came back to see me about six months after our first meeting. She said she enjoyed showing off her new Picasso—and I want to emphasize I never handled, never even saw that painting—but that she had another problem. A friend of hers had admired the Picasso and was interested in buying one, but wanted to see documentation regarding the purchase price."

"Did she mention this friend's name?" I asked, thinking it must have been Tiffany.

"No," he said. "Well, not at that point anyway. Anne offered to pay me a substantial fee to write her a receipted invoice for $625,000 on stationery from the Redburn. I took the money—cash. I'm not proud of it, but really, I thought, what difference does it make if some woman from Ohio has a piece of paper to wave around so she can show how much she paid for a painting. It wasn't as if I was actually selling a forgery or handling enough money to pay for a Picasso."

No, I thought, you were only compromising your reputation and the reputation of your employer.

I found my photo of Tiffany's Picasso on my phone and showed it to him. "Do you know anything about this painting?"

The color drained from his face. "This is where things turned really bad. Almost a year and a half ago another woman from Ohio came to see me . . ."

"Tiffany Milman?" I asked.

Jappling's face went slack. He had no more hope of keeping secrets. "Yes. She came to me, wanting to buy a painting like Anne's. Naturally I told her I had none and doubted she would find anything similar on the market."

"And yet, somehow, Tiffany Milman bought one, and she says she got hers from the Redburn Gallery too."

Jappling started to stand. "I need water. My throat is dry."

"Finish your story," said Pat.

Jappling sat and swallowed hard. "Anne came to my office again and said she had arranged to buy another forgery and that she wanted me to sell it to Tiffany Milman through the Redburn as a genuine Picasso. I told her that was ridiculous and that she should have her friend do the same thing she did. She refused, saying her whole point was to trick this other woman into buying a fake."

Jappling paused as if expecting I would have questions, but the entire scheme was clear to me. Anne Ghent bought a forgery and then persuaded Jappling to document its sale, all for the purpose of luring Tiffany into paying full price for a second forgery. I had never heard of such an elaborate and expensive practical joke.

"And what did you tell Anne Ghent?" I asked.

"When I said I would have nothing to do with it, she reminded me she had a receipt from the Redburn with my name on it for a fake painting. She said if I didn't do as she asked, she would go to the police with a complaint that I had defrauded her. I argued with her, but it didn't matter. Once I thought about it, I realized, if that receipt ever came to light, the gallery would want to know what I did with the $625,000 I supposedly collected from Anne Ghent for her Picasso.

"So, then you did as Anne wanted and sold a fake to Tiffany Milman?"

Jappling nodded. "It was the worst day of my life when I gave in to Anne Ghent's blackmail. When the forgery was ready, I hung it in the gallery, and contacted Tiffany Milman. She came here, glanced at it, and wrote me a check for the full amount."

"How long ago was this?"

"A bit over a year ago.

That meant that for more than a year the two fake Picassos had hung in their respective homes. No doubt their owners had shown them off and guests had admired them. All the while Anne enjoyed knowing she had made a fool of Tiffany. "Was that the last you heard from Anne Ghent?" I asked.

Jappling bowed his head, apparently too weary to hold it up any longer. "I thought that would be the end of it, but Anne came to see me last fall, saying she wanted to sell her fake Picasso. She expected me to put it on the walls here and sell it to someone for full price."

"What did you tell her?"

"I knew she wouldn't take no for an answer, but I stalled, hoping I could somehow get out of this nightmare. And I did. You called me with the news Anne had been killed and demanded to know the provenance so her husband could sell the painting. I made up the story I told you about a family who got the painting directly from Picasso. It was plausible. Owners often sell anonymously. If you had just accepted that, and helped Anne's husband sell the painting, all this could have been avoided."

That set a new standard for wishful thinking. "Do you mean you would have sold Anne's fake to some unsuspecting person?"

"It's not as if that never happened before."

"And now there's another one hanging downstairs," I said.

Jappling's face went blank for a moment before he gasped. "Oh, right, you saw that. Yes. Apparently, there is to be no end to my humiliation. Six months ago, the owners of the gallery said they were so impressed with the big sale I made to Tiffany Milman that they encouraged me to scour the market for more obscure Picassos. For a while, I made excuses. Then I started looking for legitimate paintings to sell, but it's a tough market. I couldn't come up with another in that price range.

"Then, the owners implied that unless I could come up with another big sale they would replace me as sales director. So, I called restorers, saying the Redburn had occasional need to repair paintings and I wanted to know their specialties. Over lunch or coffee I would make a joke about forgeries, and see if the person would return the joke. The process is a lot like picking someone up in a bar. You don't come right out and ask if they will do it. You just see who is most comfortable talking about it. I think I may have ended up with the same forger Anne used."

"But you could have called Anne and offered to sell her painting. Why didn't you?"

"Because I knew she would find some way to use it against me. I couldn't stand the thought of being involved with that woman any further."

My head was spinning from Jappling's wild tale, and I had to get back to my purpose in meeting with him. I needed to bring a letter back to John Ghent to get reimbursed for this trip. Otherwise, I would be carrying a balance on my credit card for the next few months.

"Mr. Jappling, I need a signed letter from you . . ."

"No! I can't," he said. "If all this comes out, I'll never work again. I won't even be able to get a job as a cashier in a museum store. Please! At least let me resign here and leave town. I'll disappear, move back to Madison, Wisconsin. I promise you I'll never be involved in anything like this again."

"Mr. Jappling, hear me out. I need a letter signed by you saying you did not give Anne Ghent a provenance at the time she bought her Picasso. That much is true, so there's no harm in putting it in writing. You don't have to say why you didn't.

"I will deliver this letter to her husband, John Ghent, and he can do as he likes with the painting. If he wants to sell it, it will be up to him to pay for expert opinions regarding its authenticity. If he has a letter saying no one at the Redburn knew anything about the painting at the time Anne bought it, I don't see why he or anyone else would come here asking questions."

Jappling looked as if he'd rather drop dead than answer me.

"Will you write this letter?" I asked.

Jappling sat so long with his eyes boring into the top of his desk I began to wonder if he had heard me.

Finally, he said, "Alright."

He opened the laptop on his desk and typed a few lines. When he closed the laptop, he said, "I'll have to pick it up from the printer in the other room."

"I'll go with you," said Pat.

Alone, I stood and stretched to release the tension that built up in me during this conversation.

When two sets of footsteps sounded in the corridor, I began to feel eager to get away from the Redburn Gallery.

Jappling came in and handed me the letter. I scanned it to make sure it said what I wanted it to say. I folded it into its envelope and put it in my purse.

"Thank you for your time, Mr. Jappling," I said as I walked to the door.

"Please don't say anything about this," said Jappling.

"I'll come back another time to have a look at those watercolors," said Pat.

"If you do, you can talk to someone else," said Jappling. It sounded like a warning bark.

When we got to the sidewalk in front of the gallery, I said, "Let's walk over to Tenth Avenue and get a cab."

Pat nodded.

I wanted to get away from the Redburn and Mr. Lester Jappling not only because his business dealings were corrupt but also because I now knew he'd had several good reasons to kill Anne Ghent.

Chapter 26

During our cab ride uptown, Pat sat turned away from me, looking out the window at the passing buildings.

After a few minutes of silence, I said, "That was a pretty rough meeting, back there at the gallery."

Pat turned toward me, shook his head, and went back to staring out the window.

I understood we shouldn't discuss anything sensitive with the cab driver listening, but I would have appreciated some words of comfort and encouragement. I decided to hold my peace. We would have plenty of time for that conversation on the shuttle back to Newark and at the airport while we waited to board.

When we were a few blocks from Penn Station, police barriers diverted all traffic on Tenth Avenue onto neighboring streets. We asked the driver to pull over and tipped him extra for cutting the ride short. Walking the rest of the way to the station we saw that the cause was not a terrorist incident, as I had first thought, but a movie crew filming.

As we turned a corner, I asked Pat, "Do you want to get a bite in Penn Station?"

"That's fine," he said without enthusiasm.

The more I thought about it, the less eager I was to rely on the vendors at the station. When we'd arrived several hours earlier, we'd chosen a pizza place for a quick lunch because it looked better than the other offerings. That meant anything else would be a step down.

I started scanning stores as we walked north. When we

crossed 25th Street, I saw a deli on the corner.

"I'd rather pick up a few things here," I said to Pat. "Then we can eat at the station or at the airport. Do you want a sandwich?"

Without looking at me, Pat said, "Sure."

"Turkey?" I asked.

"Sounds good."

This was starting to annoy me. I don't mind doing my share of the chores, but Pat's attitude was bordering on rudeness, which wasn't like him. I guessed he was upset about the way the meeting at the gallery went. I left him waiting on the sidewalk, went in, and bought our food.

With a bag full of sandwiches, salads, candy bars, and bottled drinks, we arrived at Penn Station in time to catch an airport shuttle leaving earlier than the one we'd planned. Since it's better to be early for a flight than late, we took it.

As we rode to the airport, in an effort to start some sort of conversation, I asked, "Do you have term papers to grade?"

"A few," said Pat.

"How about exams?"

"What do you mean?"

"Are you giving exams in all your classes?"

"Two of them."

I made a few more attempts to engage him on light topics before we got to the airport, but he wasn't interested.

The sandwiches, salads, and candy bars made it through security, but they confiscated our bottled drinks. After we bought replacements at a shop in the airport, I found us a table with some space around it in a food court. I was starving by then, and I guess Pat was too, because we ate in silence for a while.

With more than an hour to go before boarding, the time had come. "Pat, I need to talk to you about that session with Jappling."

"I'm sorry," he said.

"For what?"

"The violence."

I was glad to know he wasn't angry with me for dragging him along on this trip. "Thanks for bringing that up. It was a little over-the-top, but no harm done, and it did get him to spill the beans."

"It was wrong."

"Strictly speaking, I suppose it was," I said, "but you shouldn't punish yourself for it. After all, he did lay hands on me. I'm glad you stepped in."

"I could have just stopped him and told him not to do that. I didn't have to hurt him."

"Okay. That's a good point. Can we just say 'lesson learned,' and 'it won't happen again?'"

"No. It will happen again."

That took my breath away. "It will? Why?"

"I have PTSD."

I mentally scanned my memories of our conversations over the last sixteen months. "You never said anything about being in the military."

"I wasn't. There are other kinds of trauma."

"Right, but do they also give you this disorder?"

"Any kind of trauma that is severe and prolonged will do it, or one that happens when you're young, as mine did."

I'd been intimate with this man for more than a year and had never heard anything about his having a difficult childhood. I didn't know what to think. "What happened?'

"My dad abused us."

I felt numb all over. "How? What did he do?"

"He hit us, my sister and me. My mom too."

I pulled a package of tissue from my purse and wiped tears from my eyes. When I reached out to squeeze his hand, he let me, but he didn't squeeze back.

"Were you badly hurt?" I asked.

"Never bad enough to draw attention. It went on for years. We lived in terror. Terror became normal."

I had to reach for more tissues so I could mop my cheeks.

"Do you still feel scared all the time?" I asked.

"Usually not, but certain things bring it back. They're called triggers. If I see a man in his forties getting really drunk, I'll start to shake. A part of me feels like I'm ten years old again and the hitting is about to start. That part takes over. That becomes my reality."

"Did something happen back at the gallery to make you afraid?"

"There are different triggers. When Jappling put his hands on your shoulders, he triggered a rage inside me, and I felt justified in attacking him. I didn't even think about it. I acted on instinct, like when a car turns a corner and you run to get out of the crosswalk. It was only afterward, as we left the building, I remembered Dad laying hands on my sister."

I took a moment to blow my nose and dry my eyes. I took his hand again and squeezed, but there was still no response. "You can't control this. You're not responsible for what happened with Jappling."

"I am responsible for taking precautions."

"What precautions can you take?"

He closed his eyes and held still for a moment. "I don't think I can talk about this anymore. I'm feeling hollowed out. I need to rest."

"Of course," I said. His face had gone slack, and he spoke in a monotone. This was not the man I knew.

We moved to the seating area around the gate for our flight. I tried to get going on a paperback I'd brought with me, but I kept thinking about what Pat had just told me. I knew PTSD stood for post-traumatic stress disorder. I'd thought it was something only combat veterans had, but obviously I was wrong. I remembered that when I met him over a year ago, he mentioned his research on organized hate groups had something to do with PTSD.

Pat's description of his triggers and how they work was terrifying. You would think you were coping with a difficult situation and only later recognize your actions were inappropriate. It would be as if you momentarily fought with ghosts. Then the ghosts disappeared and you were fighting with a real person who reminded you of the ghosts.

I didn't think I could live like that, but somehow Pat managed. Maybe his precautions worked most of the time. This time, however, they didn't, and he saw that as a failure to take responsibility. That thought brought tears to my eyes again.

It seemed like there had to be some cure for people with PTSD, but as a psychologist Pat would have known about it if there were and would have sought treatment.

I needed a lot more information, and he was the best source, but he'd already told me he couldn't talk about it just now, so I would have to wait. As soon as he was feeling better, I would ask him all about it and find a way to help him live with it. In the meantime, it broke my heart to see the strong, smart, sexy man I loved looking defeated.

Our flight to Columbus and drive to campus went like clockwork. We focused on getting home safely and, at Pat's insistence, postponed all other thoughts, feelings, and conversations.

Alone in my Rabbit Hutch, I went through the motions of getting ready for bed, but two thoughts kept nagging at me. I had to report my conversation with Lester Japping to law enforcement, and I had to turn Jappling's letter over to John Ghent and be done with that business. It was too late to call the Shawville Police Department, so I focused on the second. It was after nine o'clock, but I called Ghent anyway.

He answered. "Good evening, professor. I hope you have some good news for me."

He sounded so lively I guessed the "orange juice" must still be flowing. "I have some information for you, John."

"Wonderful! Come on over, and we can have a drink and talk about it."

"It's too late for me to make the trip to Shawville. Could

you meet me tomorrow afternoon at four? There's a coffee shop in a shopping center, a little ways south of the funeral home where you held Anne's memorial service."

"There's no need for that. Why don't you just drop by the house?"

"I think you know why, John."

He was silent so long I began to wonder whether he was able to connect what I was saying with the remarks he had made to me Saturday afternoon, but when he spoke his grim tone suggested he was. "Alright then, professor, have it your way. I know the place you're talking about. I'll see you there, and you'd better not be late. And you'd better have good news."

He hung up without waiting for a reply.

Despite his confrontational attitude, I felt calm as I put down my phone.

I tucked myself in, and had no trouble falling asleep.

Chapter 27

Monday morning, over breakfast, I went online and read all the news reports posted so far about Anne Ghent's murder. They all described the murder as an armed robbery gone bad. There had been no change in the direction of the investigation, despite my conversation with Detective Murphy. The Shawville Police Department continued to focus on Tyrell Johnson of Wickwood as the prime suspect.

Perhaps that would change when I told Murphy that Anne Ghent had given Lester Jappling several reasons to kill her.

I called the department, asked to speak to Murphy, and went on hold for a minute.

"This is Detective Murphy." He sounded sleepy.

"Good morning, Detective. This is Nicole Tang Noonan."

"Good morning, Professor. What can I do for you?"

"I met someone over the weekend who had a reason to kill Anne Ghent."

Murphy fortified himself with a deep breath before asking, "Why do you think this person would have wanted to murder Mrs. Ghent?"

"They were involved in some dishonest business dealings and she threatened to expose him."

"I see. What is this person's name?"

"I would prefer to speak to you in person."

"That's really not necessary. If you'll just give me the information . . ."

"I'm not available tomorrow, but I could come to the police station on Tuesday."

We compared schedules and agreed I would come to the police department in Shawville on Tuesday afternoon to meet with him.

With that decided, I faced the cold reality of setting aside the ongoing drama surrounding these paintings and taking up the routine chores of a college professor. Along with classes to teach, I had exams to plan, and papers to grade. One paper in particular, Elaine Wiltman's, remained ungraded. I didn't have anything at stake there, so far as I knew, but I hated waiting for an answer from the deans when I didn't even understand what the question was.

And then there was the gallery. A glance at my calendar told me it was only last Wednesday that I proposed to the Gallery Advisory Committee an artist to take the place of Mira Robillard for our fall exhibit, though it seemed like months ago. At that meeting, Shirley and Greta joined forces to stall the process, and Bert ducked the issue. I needed his support to break the deadlock so I could write to the artist.

I started to look up Bert's class schedule and office hours so I could find a time to talk with him but remembered I had once seen him at the espresso bar on campus around nine thirty. Perhaps, like me, he was in the habit of dropping by for coffee before morning classes. It was worth a try. I could always look him up later.

I got to the espresso bar by nine fifteen, bought a latte and a biscotti, and took a stool at a tall table in the corner where I could keep an eye out for Bert.

Traffic increased steadily as nine thirty approached, but the baristas kept up with demand. The line for orders was never more than four deep, and a similar number waited for drinks to arrive.

I saw Bert pick up his drink from the near end of the counter. Even at a distance he was recognizable by his tidy haircut. It had to be a toupee. I waited while he stirred something into it and called to him as he walked toward the door.

He paused and scanned the tables on my side of the room with eyebrows raised and a pleasant expression on his face. I waved. He saw me, and his face fell. He looked at the door, glanced at me, and called out "Good morning," before continuing on his way.

"Bert! Can you sit down a minute?"

He hesitated. I'd been loud enough to draw stares from the tables around me, so he couldn't pretend he didn't hear me. As he walked to the stool across the table from me, he glanced at the adjacent tables and checked his watch. "Just for a minute," he said. "I've got class at ten."

"So do I," I replied.

He put his coffee on the table, sat, and put on his poker face.

"I checked with Hassan Shebib," I said.

He looked confused.

"His sculptures are between two and five pounds," I continued. "That's including the wooden base which is integral to each piece."

"Ah," he said, nodding. "Well, that's fine then."

"So, can I count on your support for moving ahead with the exhibit?"

He pursed his lips and shrugged. "I suppose so. You don't need our permission. The committee's largely symbolic, isn't it?"

"I suppose, but symbols are important. What's wrong? Earlier this year, you seemed to enjoy being on the committee. Since that last meeting you seem not to want to have anything to do with it."

"End of the school year, I suppose," he said. "I guess I'm running out of energy." He glanced at his watch. "I have to go."

"I'll walk with you," I said. "I've never seen your office. Which floor is it on?"

He stopped next to the table. "That's not necessary."

"Of course not. I know that, but what's the objection?

Seriously, Bert, what is going on?"

Again, he scanned the adjacent tables as if concerned about who might overhear us.

"You should know, Nicole, you're not making any friends in the School of Business with the way you're handling Elaine Wiltman's paper."

Even Bert had heard about this. "I wasn't aware that the purpose of grading papers was to make friends among the faculty," I said, sounding as ironic as I could.

"I wouldn't joke about it if I were you," he said. "There's a lot at stake."

"Like what? Help me out here, Bert. Last Friday I had a meeting with my dean and your dean. Your dean questioned me about how I handle instances of plagiarism, which was strange since I'm not currently handling an instance of plagiarism."

"That's not what Bayliss thinks and that's not the story going around with the business faculty."

There was a story going around. "All I've done is tell Elaine Wiltman she has to document the source on which her paper is obviously based. I never said anything about plagiarism."

"Somebody did because her parents are threatening to sue the school."

So, Pat guessed right. "Then it's a misunderstanding, Bert. Why didn't Bayliss try to work it out instead of coming at me with guns blazing?"

"It's not that simple," said Bert. "Elaine Wiltman received the Lufton Scholarship."

"So what? Most students receive some form of financial aid."

Bert shook his head. "The Lufton family were major donors for the School of Business and they endowed this scholarship. When Elaine Wiltman was chosen as the first recipient, they had a ceremony and took a photo of her with Mr. and Mrs. Lufton in the atrium. How's it going to play if

Elaine is expelled for plagiarism?"

"Expelled? This is crazy. Why is anyone even saying that? How does 'Add a footnote' get turned into 'expelled for plagiarism?'"

"I don't know, but you'd better hope they manage to keep this under wraps." He glanced at his watch. "I have to go."

I was stunned. To jump-start my brain, I reviewed what had happened and saw that up to now none of this made sense. It made no sense when Elaine refused to add a footnote and refused to speak to me. It made no sense when two deans got involved in a routine matter between a professor and a student. And it made no sense when one of them, Oscar Bayliss, accused me of failing to teach my students about plagiarism.

But now it all made sense. The Lufton's were vital to the School of Business. Elaine won the Lufton Scholarship; therefore she could do no wrong. If she had done something that could be construed as plagiarism, it must be my fault. No doubt Bayliss was congratulating himself on being proactive about protecting a source of funding.

Where did that leave me? Dean Krupnik said she called the meeting because she and Bayliss wanted to be informed of what was happening, and that she would be in touch if they had any further questions. With less than three weeks before the end of the semester, time was growing short for grading that paper. Knowing Elaine Wiltman was the golden girl of the School of Business, I wasn't inclined to force the matter, but neither could I rewrite the rules of scholarship for her. I would have to talk about this with my chairman, Frank Rossi.

I noticed I had two minutes to get to my first section of Art Appreciation and ran out of the cafe.

Chapter 28

I'd made the trip up Route 35 so many times recently I had it memorized. When a certain forest interrupted the rolling farmland, I knew I would see a white farmhouse and its adjacent sheds when I was past the trees. As I climbed toward the crest of a certain hill, I knew there would be an interchange with a gas station on the other side.

Still, spring kept me entertained. We had nothing like it in the San Francisco Bay Area, where I grew up. In Ohio, the natural world goes from months of looking like a black-and-white photograph to showing small eruptions of color with crocuses, daffodils, and redbud trees. As they reach full stage, buds appear on the deciduous trees, lending the canopy a wispy lime color. As I drove up to Shawville on that day in early May, the world around me had begun to settle into the deep green that would persist until fall, and the forsythia was running riot with its flaming yellow blossoms.

I felt more mellow than I had any right to as I walked into the coffee shop and found John Ghent waiting for me. I bought an herb tea and sat across from him.

"What do you have for me?" he said.

I took the envelope containing Jappling's letter from my purse and handed it to him.

He pulled it out and read it. "This doesn't do me any good."

"I think it does," I replied. "Knowing Anne did not get a clear provenance when she bought the painting, you should take precautions before offering the painting for sale. You'll

169

need to consult someone who specializes in Picasso. I can give you some numbers to call. Once you have a professional description and appraisal, you can sell it without worrying that you'll end up in a dispute about its authenticity."

Ghent scowled at the letter and rubbed the edge of it between his thumb and forefinger as if further testing its quality. "I don't believe it. You're saying Anne bought a painting without knowing where it came from. This is not the Anne I know. I've seen her interrogate gallery owners as if she was trying to convict them of a crime. She once went into a pharmacy to buy cough drops and ended up sending the clerk to the stockroom for a package with a more recent expiration date. So, no, I don't believe she paid a six-figure price for a painting without knowing everything there was to know about it."

In the short time I had known John Ghent, I had never seen him so energized. At the Milmans' dinner party, at his own home, and at the memorial service, he'd let his comments slip out as if he weren't sure of what he was saying. By comparison this speech sounded like a call to arms.

"Well, John, I wasn't there, so I don't know what went on when Anne bought the painting. I have only Mr. Jappling's letter to go on."

"But you went up to New York to get this letter instead of having him send it to you."

"Given the sensitive nature of the subject, I thought it best to speak with him in person."

"What did you talk about?"

That caught me by surprise, and I had to think of something to say. "We talked about Anne's visit to the gallery, the other paintings she looked at. He said he made very clear to her that the owner of the painting offered it with no reassurances."

"You could have done that in a ten-minute phone conversation. If you want me to pay for your trip, I'll need a few more details."

"John, there weren't a lot of details. It was pretty straightforward."

"I think there's something you're not telling me."

There was a lot I wasn't telling him. I had no desire to inflict emotional pain on a man who had just lost his wife, even one who had made coarse remarks to me, but he left me no choice.

"You're right, John. Anne's dealings with Jappling were actually much more complicated," I said. "She started by asking Jappling for referrals in the art world and eventually found someone to paint a forgery. That's what she bought. Tiffany saw it in your house, admired it, and wanted to know where Anne bought it and how much it cost. So, Anne badgered Jappling into giving her a phony receipt for $625,000, a reasonable price for a Picasso in today's market. Anne also had her forger make another fake Picasso, a larger one. When Tiffany went to the Redburn and asked about buying a Picasso, Anne forced Jappling to sell the forgery to Tiffany."

John leaned across the table toward me. "How could Anne force him to do that?"

"She had that fake receipt. She could have shown it to the police and claimed Jappling cheated her. Also, the owners of the Redburn gallery would have thought Jappling pocketed the sale price."

John's jaw dropped. He sat back for a moment and stared into space. "We got a painting for the price of a forgery, and the Milmans paid full price for theirs," he said.

There was a warmth in his expression. I recalled the way Dale Milman had ridiculed John's conservative attitude toward investing at the dinner party. I couldn't blame John for taking some satisfaction from coming out ahead of his rival on this deal.

"So then," he continued, "I have a fake receipt for a fake painting. If I were to burn both of them, how much money do you think would go up in smoke?"

"I've never hired a forger, so I don't know for sure, but companies that make legitimate copies offer them for a few thousand dollars."

Ghent tipped his head back and let loose with a laugh that came all the way from his belly. I think it was the first time I'd seen him laugh.

"This is much more believable," he said. "It's nice to know what Anne was up to. Maybe I'll just keep that painting and the receipt as mementos. I'll pay your expenses. I don't mind paying for a story like that."

From my purse, I took an envelope containing my travel receipts and passed it to him. Since he was satisfied, I decided not to say anything about Anne's further scheme to sell her Picasso at market value. I would share that part of the story with Detective Brian Murphy.

Ghent stood up from the table. "Thank you, professor. It's been a pleasure doing business with you."

I nodded and said nothing. I was afraid if I opened my mouth I might vomit. I let him get to his car and drive away before I left the coffee shop.

Upon hearing about Anne's mischief toward the Milmans', John expressed affection toward her, admiration, even. That changed my impression of their relationship. He wasn't embarrassed by her cruelties at the dinner party. He loved her for them. They must have gone home afterward and laughed about how she had made everyone squirm throughout the evening.

As I drove home, I felt as if I'd strayed from my profession by getting involved with the Milmans and the Ghents. I'd spent two weeks studying a pair of forgeries. As an art historian, I would have preferred studying real works of art. On the other hand, forgery is part of the history of art. I wondered if that was a story anyone wanted to hear.

I was done with Ghent, but I still had to give Tiffany the bad news about her Picasso. When I got home, I would send her an email and set up a meeting for the coming week.

On Tuesday, I had yogurt and a banana in my office after my morning class while looking up directions to the police station in Shawville. Before leaving I glanced at my inbox and saw an email from the dean of liberal arts, Vera Krupnik. It read:

> Dean Bayliss and I have reviewed the circumstances surrounding the dispute over Elaine Wiltman's term paper for your course, Modern Art. Nothing we have learned suggests any impropriety in your handling of the matter. However, having spoken with Ms. Wiltman, we believe she understands the necessity of citing sources, and we recommend you grade the paper as if citation were not an issue in this instance. We thank you for your cooperation.

Everything about this email was wrong. The word "dispute" was wrong. There was no dispute. Everything was plain as day. Like every other scholar, she needed to acknowledge her source.

Krupnik's attempt to reassure me by saying, "Nothing we have learned suggests any impropriety," was wrong. No reasonable person would have seen any impropriety in what I did.

The discovery by the deans that Wiltman "understands the necessity of citing sources" was irrelevant. Understanding is not enough. She needed to go ahead and cite them.

Most profoundly wrong was their recommendation that I grade the paper "as if citation were not an issue in this instance." In other words, pretend it never happened.

Actually, it was much worse than that. Based on what Bert Stemple had told me, they were asking me to lie so they could appease parents threatening to sue the school. It was as if

Vera Krupnik was saying to me, "All our troubles will go away, Nicole, if you'll just tell this one little lie." How courageous of them: willing to use my lie to repair their failure to communicate.

The hell I would! That one little lie would turn my work with my students into one big lie. If Elaine Wiltman's parents could squeal "not our daughter," then why should anyone's son or daughter be held to academic standards? Why should I demand good work from students whose parents did not threaten a lawsuit when things didn't go their way? Why teach?

Knowing I would fire off an angry email if I sat at the keyboard any longer, I walked down the hall to Frank Rossi's office. The situation called for action from my department chairman. Professors shouldn't have to deal with deans.

The lights were off in Frank's office and there was a note on his door, which said, "Dr. Rossi's classes and office hours are cancelled today." Frank might have been down with the flu or off to some appointment, medical or otherwise. But, the way things were going, this felt like some invisible hand was squeezing me a little harder, making my life a little more difficult, keeping me from doing my job with purpose and integrity.

Breathing exercises helped me get my mind off that track as I walked back to my office. I could wait until tomorrow to talk to Frank. Once I had his perspective, I could decide how to respond to Krupnik's memo.

While walking back to my Rabbit Hutch, I remembered it had been two days since I'd talked to Pat. He had said he needed time to himself, and I had respected that, but enough was enough. When I got inside, I called him. "Hey, babe, how you doing?"

"About the same."

"Is that good or bad?"

After a few seconds, he said, "It is what it is."

"Let me be more direct. Should I come over there and

make sure you're wearing clean clothes and eating regular meals?"

I was glad to hear him laugh at that.

"You don't need to worry about me. I've dealt with this before. I have people I can call about this, and I have called them. I don't make the mistake of trying to deal with it by myself."

"I'm glad to hear it. I'll be off campus most of this afternoon. How about if I pick up a pizza in Blanton on my way back and bring it over to your place? Maybe around six?"

He sighed. "Can you give me another day or two? I want to talk to you about all this, but I'm not quite ready."

"If you say so, but you'd better not be fooling me."

"Not a chance. I put on clean underwear this morning. Cross my heart."

"Oh, thanks a lot! Now I'm going to be thinking about you in your underwear until I see you again. Don't make me wait too long."

"I'll call you."

I knew Pat would be okay. I could hear warmth and humor in his voice that hadn't been there when I'd seen him on Sunday. That gave me courage as I started my drive to Shawville to tell Detective Brian Murphy about Lester Jappling.

Chapter 29

Shawville's police station was a one-story, flat-roofed, brick building surrounded by a parking lot on a plot of land carved out of a stand of scrub trees. It had an entrance at one end and not enough windows for its size. Without much effort, it could have been turned into a small shopping center. I was surprised to see so little had gone into a civic building in a city full of upscale malls, country clubs, and grand homes on sweeping lawns.

The officer at the front desk walked me to Detective Murphy's desk. I declined the offer of soda or coffee.

Murphy wasn't much over forty, with thick brown hair showing only a few strands of silver. In his corduroy jacket, denim shirt and wool pants, he could have passed for a college professor.

"Professor Noonan, have a seat," he said, as he took out a pad of paper and clicked his ballpoint pen. "I believe you said Anne Ghent was involved in some shady business dealings."

"That's right. This goes back a couple of years and was still going on until a couple of weeks ago. Anne Ghent paid someone to paint a picture that looked like it might be by Picasso and put Picasso's signature on it. She bought a forgery. Then, a year-and-a-half ago, she went to a gallery and got an employee to write her a receipt to show she had paid $625,000 for it."

From the way Murphy was squinting, I could tell this was new territory for him. "Why would someone at a gallery do that?" he asked.

"She could be very persuasive."

"What is this employee's name?"

"Lester Jappling."

"And what was the name of the gallery?"

"Redburn Gallery."

Murphy jotted all this information on his pad as he asked, "In Columbus?"

"No, in New York."

"New York City?"

I nodded.

He stared across the room at nothing in particular for a moment, before jotting "NYC" on his pad. "And how do you know that Ms. Ghent got this receipt from Mr. Jappling?"

"I went to New York on Sunday and spoke with Mr. Jappling at the Redburn Gallery. That is what he told me."

"Why did you go there to talk to him?"

"I've been working with John Ghent. He wants to sell his late wife's collection of paintings."

Murphy reviewed what he'd written on his pad. "From what you've told me so far, neither of them committed a crime," he said. "Did either of them sell this forgery, claiming it was by Picasso?"

"About nine months ago, Anne Ghent came to Jappling and said she wanted him to do exactly that: Sell the painting on consignment through the Redburn Gallery for as much as it would command in the current market."

"And what did Jappling do?"

"He refused, but she threatened to show the receipt he had signed to the police and to the owners of the gallery. Basically, she was going to accuse Jappling of selling her a forgery."

Murphy smiled, appreciating the irony. "So, she had him in a corner."

"Yes, and there's a little more to it. A little over a year ago, she bought another forgery and again used that same fake receipt to force Jappling to sell it through the Redburn to Tiffany Milman for the full price of a Picasso."

Murphy hummed while he jotted. "So, they conspired to defraud Ms. Milman."

"That's right."

Again, Murphy read over his notes. "Just to be clear, Dr. Noonan, in your view how does this relate to the murder of Anne Ghent?"

"I think it gave Lester Jappling a reason to kill her. Twice she threatened to ruin his career if he wouldn't join her in committing fraud. When I spoke to him on Sunday, he was clearly frustrated—frantic, really. He said when she came to him the last time—that is, when she wanted him to sell her forgery through the gallery—he couldn't stand the thought of being involved with her any further."

Murphy scratched the back of his head while reading over his notes again. "Dr. Noonan, the murder of Anne Ghent was a brutal crime. She was gunned down in the parking lot of a shopping mall. It's hard for me to imagine a guy who works at an art gallery in New York doing something like this. Do you understand what I'm saying? I think we're dealing with a different class of people here."

I wasn't sure what Murphy meant by "class of people," but I didn't like the sound of it. "I'm sure Lester Jappling is perfectly capable of pulling a trigger."

"I'm sure he is," said Murphy. "But it's the psychology that concerns me. Most people, when they have a problem, don't decide to solve it by picking up a gun and shooting somebody, even if it's a serious problem like this one." He clicked his pen a few times, as if punctuating his remarks.

"Detective, if you had seen the state Jappling was in when I questioned him about all this, you would have believed he was willing to kill. And on top of these other frauds, there is a third forgery hanging on the wall at the Redburn right now, or at least there was on Sunday. He said the gallery pressured him to make another big sale, so he bought another fake. He was willing to do that rather than sell Anne Ghent's forgery because he couldn't stand the idea of having further dealings with her."

Murphy made another note. "I can alert the police in New York to these cases of fraud. Really, though, it sounds like Jappling was ending things with Ms. Ghent without resorting to violence."

"But she had the power to ruin him any time."

"Dr. Noonan, think of the practical side of this. Ms. Ghent was shot in the parking lot of a mall not too far from here. Mr. Jappling works in Manhattan, so he probably lives in New York, maybe New Jersey. Do you think he would travel across the state of Pennsylvania and half the state of Ohio, and somehow could know where Ms. Ghent would be in a very large parking lot, at a particular time, so he could shoot her? It doesn't make sense."

"Maybe he didn't actually pull the trigger."

Murphy had a smirk on his face as he said, "You think he hired a hit man? No. That's in the movies. Nobody outside of organized crime has the ability to put out a contract on somebody they don't like. Think about it: If there was somebody at your university, who was making your life miserable, would you know how to hire someone to kill them?"

Murphy didn't know how close he was to describing my situation with the deans.

"Of course not," he continued. "This was a crime of opportunity. The man we have in custody has a history of petty crime. He was in that parking lot, looking for a soft target, to make a quick score. This time it got out of hand."

"So, because he had a history of petty crime, you think Tyrell Johnson did it?"

"Yes."

"And because he comes from a different class of people?"

Murphy's face hardened several degrees. "I don't like what you're implying. We've got the right man. Thank you for coming in today, Dr. Noonan. We appreciate your cooperation. I'll walk you out."

We didn't speak as we walked to the front desk.

"Thanks, again," said Murphy as he left me at the desk, but he didn't sound like he meant it.

Familiar though I was with the drive between Shawville and my campus, I paid extra attention to the road signs and mileage markers because I couldn't stop thinking about what had just happened. Murphy refused to take seriously Jappling's motive for killing Anne Ghent because he thought violent crime was committed by "a different class of people." I was pretty sure he meant people from Wickwood, black people.

Murphy was right about one thing though. It wasn't clear how Jappling could have done it. That meant someone had to find out where Jappling was when Anne Ghent was shot and find out if he had an alibi. If he was in New York, and people saw him there, he was in the clear. If not, someone had to investigate whether Jappling could have traveled to Shawville, found her, and killed her.

That sounded like a job for the police. If they didn't do their job, I would have to think of something else. I couldn't go back to my comfortable life as a college professor, read the news reports about the wheels of justice crushing Tyrell Johnson, and say to my friends, not to mention the donors I was trying to develop, "Such a shame!"

Maybe I could write a letter to the editor of Shawville's newspaper protesting the police department's failure to follow a promising lead. There were only two problems with that plan. I didn't know if Shawville had a newspaper, and I doubted the city that separated itself from Wickwood wanted to know about their police failing to look elsewhere for a suspect.

I needed help deciding what to do about my suspicions regarding Jappling. I decided to call Mason Adams, sheriff of Payne County, who had investigated past murders connected to my campus. More than two years ago, we had started on the wrong foot, but we had come to respect one another. I doubted he could get directly involved in this investigation, but I hoped he could help me understand my options.

Chapter 30

I caught up with Frank Rossi in his office around lunchtime on Wednesday. He had departed from his usual, colorful clothes by wearing a black blazer and gray slacks with a black-and-white striped shirt.

"Nicole. Have a seat. Ready to wrap up the semester?"

"Almost," I said. "Do you remember when I told you I'd been called to a meeting with the deans of liberal arts and business?"

"Right. How did that go?"

"Krupnik said they wanted to be informed about the situation. Bayliss questioned me about how I handled plagiarism."

Frank looked confused. "Plagiarism?"

"I know. I never said anything about plagiarism to my student. I wasn't sure why Bayliss brought it up. Then, this morning, I got this." I handed him a printed copy of Krupnik's email.

After reading it, Frank said, "Well, then, false alarm. No plagiarism." He put the email on his desk where I could reach it.

"Frank, they're suggesting I ignore all this and grade the paper."

Frank shrugged. "Lets you off the hook."

"I wasn't on the hook. They're saying I should give her a grade without first making her put a citation on the paper."

Frank glanced at the email again. "Right. Says the student understands about that now."

"So why wouldn't she just write the citation on the last page?"

Frank shrugged.

"I don't feel right about giving a student credit for something she didn't do."

Frank pointed to the email. "It's on them, not you."

"I'm not worried about who will get blamed. I think it's the wrong thing to do."

Frank stared past me, as if he were pondering some eternal mystery. "Up to you," he said.

I took the printed copy of the dean's email from the desk and folded it so I wouldn't have to look at Krupnik's words. "I talked to Bert Stemple Monday morning. He's on the Gallery Advisory Committee."

Frank smiled and nodded.

I went on. "He's been very friendly all year, but he wasn't so friendly this time. When I asked him what was wrong, he said the story going around the business school is that I accused Elaine Wiltman of plagiarism, therefore her parents are threatening to sue the school, and the dean is freaking out because she won the Lufton scholarship, which is named after a big donor."

Frank looked relieved. "There you are, then."

"What do you mean? Where am I?"

"This isn't about Elaine's paper or you. They can't have the parents suing the school, and they can't look bad to the donors."

I took a deep breath and relaxed so I wouldn't be too loud when I replied. "Why couldn't the dean have explained to the parents that I'm not accusing their daughter of plagiarism? No one is."

Frank shrugged.

I recalled Pat's guess that some classmate had told Elaine she could be accused of plagiarism. So long as that remained a possibility in Elaine's mind, she wouldn't say anything to anyone, especially since she probably had paid someone to write the paper in the first place. And so long as Elaine was screaming, "she's accusing me of plagiarism," her parents would defend her like a mama bear defends her cub. And so long as they threatened to sue, everyone would give them whatever they wanted.

I stood up. "Thanks for talking this over with me."

Frank smiled. "Anytime."

I walked back to my office on wobbly legs, hung my jacket on the hook I had added above the little window in the door so no one could see in, and locked the door. With my desk chair pulled up to the window that took up most of one wall in my office, I feasted my eyes on the pastel colors of spring as they played out on the hillside that descended from behind the building and the woods that spread beyond it.

This view had been a great comfort to me throughout my three years on this campus. I had watched the velvet green of summer turn to the fiery colors of autumn, which in turn became the black and white of naked trees on a snowy field, before yielding the pastels of spring.

By the time I finished my survey of spring's progress, I had regained my composure. I now understood that the values of this academic community had been revealed to me by the deans and confirmed by Frank Rossi. No one else saw anything wrong with what was happening. In this place it was not considered wrong to give a student unearned credit for the purpose of pacifying defensive parents.

If I graded the paper as my dean instructed, I would always feel like a fraud. If I refused, I would become one of those whistleblowers whom everyone admires, and no one supports.

I flipped through the files in my desk drawer, took out Elaine's paper, and placed it in the middle of my desktop. From my backpack, I got the green pen I used for marking students' papers and exams.

It wasn't my job to reform the school. They paid me to teach, and if their definition of teaching included compromising on a grade, then it was my job to compromise. It was not the job I wanted, but it was the job they paid me to do.

I turned to the last page of Elaine's paper and was ready to grade it when I had another thought. I returned my green pen to my backpack, and found a red marker in my desk drawer. I used it to write a big red A.

I got to my classroom a few minutes early for Modern Art and kept busy sorting slides on my laptop while the students arrived in ones and twos. Elaine Wiltman arrived on the hour. I walked back to where she was sitting, held out her paper, and said, "Sorry for the misunderstanding," hoping to defuse the situation.

She gave it a wary glance and took it.

I went back to the front of the room and started my lecture on later twentieth-century art movements that reflected back to the classical tradition from which modern art had departed.

As I warmed to the subject, I noticed Elaine Wiltman holding her paper with the pages flipped so the last one was showing. She looked to her right and turned the paper toward her friend sitting across the aisle. That student suppressed her smile and gave Elaine a thumbs-up.
Elaine smiled back.

I finished class on auto-pilot and walked as fast as I could back to my Rabbit Hutch, looking forward to the trip into Blanton for my meeting with Sheriff Mason Adams. Perhaps a conversation with him would remind me there was still such a thing as right and wrong in the world.

Chapter 31

Sheriff Mason Adams had agreed to meet me at Emma's deli in Blanton. The spring weather allowed us to take an umbrella table on the sidewalk in front. I hadn't seen the sheriff in over a year, and I was impressed all over again by the easy way he carried himself. He stood head and shoulders above me, and never seemed off balance. He was probably ten years older than me and had the physique of a younger man.

After putting his cup of coffee on the table, he took care getting himself settled on the folding chair opposite me, took off his campaign hat, and rested it on another chair. "How are things at the university?" he asked.

I thought about describing the opening of the School of Business, efforts being made to manage the increase in enrollment, and the outlook for changes of curriculum, but I remembered not to take his question literally. "Just fine," I said. "We're about to wrap up the semester."

Adams nodded.

I took his silence as a cue to get on with it. "I've been meeting with two families who live over in Shawville. They both have art collections, and, to make a long story short, they each have a painting that's supposed to be by Picasso, but is really a forgery."

Adams looked surprised, but said nothing.

I continued: "This past Sunday, I made a trip to New York and talked to the sales manager of the gallery where both families bought their paintings. His name is Lester Jappling. After some prodding, he told me that one of the women deliberately bought a fake and later forced him to sell another fake to this other family for the price of a real Picasso."

Adams shook his head as if giving up on understanding the things people do. "I'm afraid this is beyond my ken," he said. "We don't run into art forgeries in Payne County. The police in New York would be your best bet."

"I understand, Sheriff, but this is all related to something more serious."

Behind me, someone called out, "Sheriff Adams! How are you on this fine day?"

I glanced over my shoulder and saw a man in jeans and a windbreaker coming our way.

"Just fine, Earl," said the Sheriff. "You say hello to your daddy for me."

"I'll do that, Sheriff." The young man glanced my way and said, "Ma'am."

I nodded back. When I suggested to the sheriff that we meet at Emma's, it hadn't occurred to me that I'd be sitting at a busy corner with one of the best-known people in the town or the county.

"Sheriff, do you remember hearing about a murder in Shawville about three weeks ago?"

He gave it serious consideration before shaking his head. "I can't say I do."

"A woman was shot in the parking lot of a mall on a Tuesday evening."

"Right. That sounds familiar."

"Her name was Anne Ghent. She was the woman I was telling you about, the one who bought a forgery and arranged for the gallery to sell her friend a forgery."

"So maybe the friend who bought the forgery found out about it, and killed her for revenge."

That brought me up short. "No. The friend doesn't know her painting is a forgery."

"How can you be sure?"

"I haven't told her. I just found out on Sunday. I have

plans to see her tomorrow, and I'll tell her then. I'm concerned about the man at the gallery. I think he might have killed Anne Ghent."

"I thought he was in on the scheme."

"Not really. It's complicated, but essentially Anne Ghent blackmailed him to go along with her scheme. When I talked to him, he blurted all this out. He seemed desperate and said he never wanted to have anything to do with her again. But she still had the means to blackmail him, so he had a motive to kill her."

The sheriff looked up and down the street for a few seconds. "Correct me if I'm wrong, but didn't the police in Shawville arrest someone for this murder?"

"Yes, a man from Wickwood, Tyrell Johnson."

"Then I suggest you find out who's leading the investigation and send that officer an email, explaining your concerns."

"Detective Brian Murphy. I talked to him yesterday. He didn't take me seriously."

Adams sat back and folded his arms. "Dr. Noonan, I'm sure you recall that you and I once disagreed about the direction of a murder investigation."

"Yes, Sheriff. That was two and a half years ago. I was impulsive and should have done a better job of consulting you."

"But, as it turned out, you were right." He smiled. "I don't know Detective Murphy, and I don't know what evidence he has. If it's fairly conclusive, he may not see any reason to open another line of investigation."

"He didn't tell me anything about the evidence."

"He wouldn't at this point."

"Sheriff, most of the people who live in Wickwood are African-American. I assume Tyrell Johnson is black. I'm wondering if Detective Murphy is just going with the most obvious suspect."

"Sometimes the simplest answer is the right one."

"And sometimes law enforcement officers act on their prejudices."

Adams frowned. "I wish I could say that wasn't true. Unfortunately, it is. However, I would be careful what you say about the detective without knowing all the facts."

I nodded. "Agreed. But, as you just mentioned, he's not giving me all the facts. So how can I make sure he or somebody else looks into Lester Jappling's motive and considers whether he's a more likely suspect.?"

Adams stared into the distance.

A man in a business suit walked by and said, "Good afternoon, Sheriff."

Adams nodded to him. "Mr. Whitaker, how's the family?"

"Just fine."

"Glad to hear it. You have a good day."

The man went on his way.

Adams turned back to me. "Let me do this: I'll run a background check on the gallery man and see if he has any history of violent crime. If he does, I'll write to Detective Murphy, telling him we talked, and forwarding the records."

"Thank you, Sheriff. I hadn't thought of that. It might turn up something. But even if it doesn't, Jappling might have killed her. This could be the first time he's done something violent."

Adams showed me his palm. "Let's see what the records say. Either way, I'll send you an email tomorrow."

I thanked him again. We said our goodbyes, and he got in his patrol car and left.

I was glad for the possibility Adams had raised but also afraid that nothing would come of it. I felt my body start to slump with the release of tension and decided to get back to campus. I hoped I might get a good night's sleep so I would be at my best when I broke the news to Tiffany that her painting was not only odd and pornographic but also a fake, and that her friend, Anne Ghent, had set her up.

As I made my fourth trip to Shawville in six days, I felt my spirits start to recover. For one thing, I was done with John Ghent. Two weeks ago, he'd called me for advice on selling Anne's paintings. Doing him that favor should have involved a few phone calls, but ended up taking Pat and me to New York where we discovered Anne's scheme to peddle fake Picassos. Since John was pleased with my report, he might even send a letter thanking me and donate some money to the university. That would be no stranger than what had already happened.

I felt uneasy about Lester Jappling still being at large. After all, if he had travelled to Ohio to kill Anne Ghent, as I suspected, he could come after me the same way. But, though I hadn't managed to put him on Detective Murphy's radar, at least I had the satisfaction of knowing Sheriff Adams might find he had a criminal record that would. For now, that was all I could do.

I didn't like the way I'd left things with Pat. I hated seeing him feeling so low. Maybe I could spend an extra night at his house this weekend. Or maybe we could go away to some place quiet and private for Friday and Saturday nights and ease the pain he felt over what he did to Jappling.

I still had no solution to the problem Dean Vera Krupnik had created by forcing me to grade Elaine Wiltman's paper. When I closed my eyes, I could still see that big red "A." I could no longer believe in the integrity of teaching at Cardinal University, but, now that Pat and I found each other, I hated the thought of leaving. Over the summer, I would consider my options.

My visit with Tiffany Millman would give me a chance to chalk up a win. Although I would have to break the news that her Picasso was a fake, I could give her some hope of recovering her money. Knowing Lester Jappling might be facing arrest, I could suggest that the Redburn might be willing to issue a refund in order to quietly separate itself from his dishonest dealings. If I presented all this in the right way, I might even continue the teacher-student relationship I had with her.

I left the freeway and followed the side roads to the driveway for Fairhaven. The pasture and the trees along the drive were greener than when Pat and I had come to dinner almost three weeks ago, and the corn was taller. As I rounded the curve where the house was revealed, I let the car coast to a stop as Pat had done that evening. Though I'd visited three times before, the house still amazed me with its size, proportions, and setting.

As on previous visits, I parked along the circle, heading away from the front door. The secretary opened the door to me, made sure all my needs were met, and left me in the drawing room. I sat on the sofa that faced the fireplace. Tiffany's Picasso still hung in the space above the mantle.

Chapter 32

Within minutes Tiffany came in and walked toward me with both arms extended. "Nicole! So good to see you."

I stood to shake hands, hug, or whatever she had in mind, but, before she got to me, she stopped, glanced at the coffee table, looked at me wide-eyed, and said, "Weren't you offered anything? Not even a glass of water?"

"Yes. Your secretary asked. I said I didn't care for anything."

Tiffany sighed and seemed disappointed. "Maybe we could have tea. It's a little early, but I think that would be nice. Would you like that? I have some macarons."

"Sure. Why not?" I said.

Tiffany wrapped me in a hug that almost lifted me off my feet before saying, "Let's sit down." She sat in the armchair, facing the couch where I sat, and tapped something into her phone, presumably the order for tea.

Her outfit was simple and elegant that day, a white silk blouse over pale blue slacks. She was, as always, made up and groomed to perfection, but this did little to hide the effects of the strain she was feeling. I remembered seeing her sobbing at the memorial service for Anne Ghent. Her friend's death had taken its toll, and, judging by her drooping eyelids and down-turned mouth, she was still feeling the loss.

"Those books you recommended arrived," she said, "but I haven't had a chance to look at them yet."

"That's alright," I said. "When you do, let me know if you have any questions."

"That's so nice. Thank you. I'll get around to them. It's just that lately it's been hard. I can't seem to concentrate. But let's not talk about me. How are you? How are things at the university?"

"We're having the usual end-of-semester panic to get everything done."

"Uh-huh. Do you stay there and teach classes in the summer too?"

"No, I go back to San Francisco and spend time with my family. That also lets me use the museums and libraries there. That way I can get some research and writing done."

Tiffany rested her head on the back of her chair and closed her eyes. "That sounds wonderful. I'd love to go away someplace and . . . I don't know . . . just look at beautiful things, and not have anything to worry about."

I glanced at her collection of art and surveyed the wood-paneled room with its French windows looking out to a garden in bloom. I couldn't imagine where she could go to improve on all this.

There was a knock at the door. A maid entered with a tea tray and set it on the coffee table in front of me. "Will there be anything else, madame?" she asked.

"Not right now," said Tiffany, as she leaned forward and pulled the tray toward her. "Cream and sugar, if I remember correctly?"

"Thank you," I said.

Once the tea was poured, I helped myself to one of the macarons. It was heavenly.

"Well, I hope you aren't spending all your time on campus," said Tiffany.

I'd been waiting until the maid had left the room to get to the subject of my visit, and Tiffany had just given me a perfect lead-in. "No, in fact I've been running lots of errands ever since John Ghent called and asked me to help him sell Anne's paintings."

Tiffany paused with her cup halfway to her lip. "Really?"

She took a sip and set the cup and saucer on the stand next to her chair. After a few moments of staring into space, she said, "That's interesting."

"He said he had other ways to remember her, and the paintings didn't really appeal to him."

Tiffany seemed lost in thought. I took another bite of my macaron and washed it down with some tea before continuing.

"I noticed something interesting the first time I went to look at her collection," I said. "There was a Picasso which is similar to yours in some ways."

Tiffany nodded. "Yes. I've seen it several times."

That confirmed what Jappling had told me about how Tiffany became interested in buying a Picasso. "I don't know if you've looked at it recently," I said, "but I noticed that, like the one you bought, it's rather sexually explicit."

"No. I hadn't noticed. Of course, it's been a while."

"When I was here a couple of weeks ago, I mentioned the explicit sexuality in your painting, and, as I recall, you were upset it about."

"Yes, I was."

"So, if it makes you feel any better, you aren't the only one who has a painting like that. In fact, many of the paintings Picasso made in his last years were quite explicit."

Tiffany sat staring into space. I didn't know what she was thinking, but I decided to plunge ahead. "I've since discovered that your Picasso and Anne's have something else in common."

Tiffany now gave me her full attention.

"I'm very sorry to tell you this, but I've learned that both your Picasso and hers are forgeries."

To my surprise, she did not react. She didn't even blink. I thought she must be having trouble taking in the implications of what I was saying.

I went on. "I visited the Redburn Gallery on Sunday and talked to Lester Jappling. He admitted that he knew Anne bought a forgery and that he gave her a receipt to make it look like she bought it from the Redburn. He also admitted that he sold you this painting," I nodded toward the one above the mantle, "knowing it too was a forgery."

"I know," said Tiffany. "Anne told me."

That was the last thing I expected to hear. I didn't know what to think, except that Tiffany could have saved me a lot of trouble if she'd mentioned this earlier.

"How long have you known?" I asked.

"A little over two weeks."

"So, you found out around the same time Anne was killed. Did you already know when I came to visit you on the Tuesday following the dinner party?"

"No. I was so shocked when you pointed out how disgusting my painting is that I wanted to talk to Anne about it." Tiffany got up and walked toward the mantle as she talked. "I called their house, and John told me she'd gone to the mall to get some shoes. I thought about calling her cell phone, but I was afraid she'd blow me off. She was like that. I don't know if you noticed. Plus, by then, I was really upset."

Tiffany stood in front of the fireplace, gazing up at the fake Picasso that hung above the mantle. "So, I drove over to the mall and cruised around the parking lots, looking for that cute little sports car she drove. When I found it, I parked a little ways off and waited for her to come out. When she did, I walked up to her and told her the Picasso I bought at the Redburn Gallery turned out to be pornographic, and did she know about that when she told me to go look at it?

"She just laughed and said, 'You think that's bad? It's also a fake.'

"I was so mad. I just stood there thinking about that day, years ago, when she got me to play in that doubles match at the tennis club. I knew I wasn't good enough to compete with Anne and her friends, but she just wouldn't let it go. 'Come on, Tiffany, you'll never get any better if you just play with beginners.' So, I played, and I pushed too hard and blew out my knee. That was the end of tennis for me.

"I stood there in that parking lot, with Anne laughing in my face, and thought about how she ruined tennis for me, and now she wanted to ruin art for me just when I was starting to become a connoisseur. That's when I remembered I had this with me."

Tiffany opened a drawer in a cabinet by the fireplace and took out a small black pistol.

"Dale got me this a few years ago and said I should always carry it for protection. I guess he thought we were so rich somebody might try to kidnap me for ransom. That is so stupid. Can you imagine me trying to hold off a couple of big guys with this little thing while they're trying to pull me into a van?"

Tiffany pointed the gun in my general direction. I heard a snap and splinters flew from the top of the coffee table in front of me.

I hit the floor and scurried toward the wall, trying to get to the door in the corner. I had the presence of mind to stay low while reaching for the door knob but gave up on escaping when I heard a second snap and splinters flew from the wood paneling next to the door.

I peeked around the corner of the sofa and saw Tiffany's aim waver. She started walking toward me while keeping the gun pointed at me.

I looked up and remembered I had my back to a wall decorated with almost a million dollars' worth of art.

I stood up, and Tiffany stopped where she was and waved her gun to the side, as if that would make me step away from her collection.

On the wall next to me was that large drawing of a reclining nude. I plucked it off its hook and held it in front of me. By crouching, I managed to make it cover me from my nose to my knees.

"Not the Matisse!" screamed Tiffany. "It cost a fortune. Dale will kill me if anything happens to it."

"Tiffany, put the gun down," I yelled.

"You know too much."

"It's not just me. Pat went to New York with me. He knows too, and he knows I'm here this afternoon."

Tiffany sighed and lowered the gun. "Well, crap."

She sat again in the armchair by the coffee table and dropped the pistol onto the tea tray.

I moved closer, keeping the drawing in front of me. "Tiffany, I swear, if you reach for that gun, I will smash this drawing over the coffee table."

"Don't worry." She slumped in the chair, her eyes ranging over her art collection.

I sat on the sofa and reached for the end of the tea tray. "I won't be able to relax while the gun is between us. I'm just going to slide this away from you."

"Don't touch it."

That didn't seem like the time to argue. "Will the maid or someone else come to find out what all the noise was?" I asked.

"No. They probably didn't hear anything. I'm sure they're all in the kitchen, eating the rest of the macarons, and gossiping about me."

"Alright then," I said, reaching for my purse on the sofa next to me. "I'll call 911. I think we have to talk to the police."

"Let's hold off on that," said Tiffany.

"I think it will look better if we call right away."

"I need to decide what to do next. I should talk to Dale."

"Where is he?"

"He's in Columbus for the day."

"What do you think Dale would want you to do?"

"I don't know," she said, sounding on the verge of throwing a tantrum. "That's why I want to talk to him."

"That's okay then," I said as softly as I could. "Maybe you could call him."

She shook her head.

"Tiffany, a little while ago, you said you wished you could go away somewhere and not have to make any decisions."

"I wasn't thinking of prison."

"Maybe it won't come to that."

Tiffany locked her eyes onto mine. "I killed Anne Ghent."

"So, you get a lawyer. He'll probably tell you not to say that to the police. Who knows what happens after that?"

"I can't go through all that," she said, eyeing the gun.

"Yes, you can. You're a strong, smart woman. Call your lawyer and follow his instructions about calling the police."

"No. Leave now."

I was not going to leave her alone with that gun. "The police have a man under arrest for the murder of Anne Ghent, a black man from Wickwood. Think about that. All he did was go to his job at the mall, and he got arrested because someone saw him in the parking lot. He had to talk to the police and talk to a lawyer. Now he's sitting in a cell. His family is going crazy, worrying about what will happen to him. Are you going to let that go on? Are you going to let him go on trial for murder?"

Tiffany had tears in her eyes.

Moving slowly, I grabbed the end of the tea tray and slid it to the far end of the coffee table, which put the gun right in front of me. I hated looking at it, so I covered it with a napkin. I set the drawing on the floor, leaning against the front of the sofa, within reach.

"Call your lawyer, now," I said.

She picked up her phone, tapped a few times, and held it to her ear.

Chapter 33

The police arrived. Lots of police. Two of them arrested Tiffany and took her away. She had been well-schooled by her lawyer not to talk to them. Others went down the corridor to the drawing room and, I assumed, to the kitchen to talk to the staff.

One officer sat with me in the reception room and interviewed me. I did my best to keep it simple, saying that, when I told Tiffany her painting was a forgery, she came out with her story about confronting Anne Ghent and killing her in a rage. That led to questions about how I knew it was a forgery, and how Anne Ghent was involved. By the time I was done answering, I'd told most of what happened at the Redburn Gallery.

The officer asked me to wait and went down the corridor. While I had a moment to myself, I checked my phone and saw a new email from Sheriff Adams. His background check had turned up no criminal record for Lester Jappling. Under the circumstances, that no longer seemed important. I tapped out a reply, thanking him, saying there had been developments, and that he should watch news reports.

After a few moments by myself, I remembered I had first sat on the same sofa almost four weeks earlier when Pat and I arrived for the Milmans' dinner party. The day after that I had emailed Tiffany, expressing interest in her Picasso. Two days later, I had visited and mentioned, among other things, the explicit sexuality in the painting. That set off a series of events that resulted in the murder of Anne Ghent within a few hours.

I knew I wasn't responsible for Anne's death. I hadn't known the sex act depicted in the painting was Anne's practical joke on Tiffany, or that Tiffany would confront Anne in a parking lot, or that Anne would mock Tiffany by telling her the painting was fake, or that Tiffany carried a pistol. But knowing I wasn't responsible didn't make me feel any better about being the rock rolling down the hillside that triggered an avalanche.

The officer who had interviewed me came back with Detective Brian Murphy. They stood outside the archway to the reception room as the officer read from her notebook and Murphy listened. After a brief conversation, the officer went outside, and Murphy joined me, sitting in a chair at the end of the coffee table.

"I understand you had a scary experience," he said.

"Yes," I replied. "Now that I think of it, this kind of thing has happened to me regularly since I moved to Ohio, though this is the first time I've been shot at."

"That's never happened to me, though somebody pointed a gun at me once. I'll be glad if that never happens again."

He took a moment to look out toward the front hall and watch some officers and technicians go by. "I guess you were right about Tyrell Johnson."

"I suppose. But I was wrong about Lester Jappling, and Curtis Diaz, and Dale Milman, and I was wrong to jump to conclusions. I could have given you the information without implying that your arrest of Tyrell Johnson was an example of bigotry."

He shrugged it off. "The important thing is you came to talk to me when you had information. The officer who took your statement tells me you came here today to talk to Mrs. Milman about her art collection."

"That's right. I thought she should know that I found out her Picasso is a fake."

"And what was her reaction?"

"She said she already knew, that Anne Ghent told her,

and that she was so angry when she heard this she took out the gun she carries for self-defense and killed her."

Murphy nodded his head slowly as if listening to an old story. "People have been killed for less."

"They had a history, Tiffany and Anne Ghent. This was not the first time Anne played a nasty practical joke on her."

Murphy leaned forward, ready to stand up. "We'll call you if we need to talk to you again. Will you be alright to drive back to Cardinal U.?"

I thought about it for a second, and decided to stop at that coffee shop for a little pick-me-up before I left Shawville. "I'll be fine."

Murphy got up, and I did to. "Thanks again," he said before he went back down the corridor.

I walked out to my car, expecting to be stopped by one of the officers who glanced at me as I walked by, but apparently there was no longer any restriction about leaving the scene of a crime.

Once I was seated at the coffee shop and had a cookie and half a cup of tea inside me, I called Pat, and he picked up. "I'll be back in about an hour," I said. "Let's have dinner. Also, I'm freaked out about what just happened at Tiffany's house. I'll tell you all about it."

"I've got some soup in the freezer. I'll start thawing it."

"That sounds great. I'll stop at Steadman's in Blanton and see if they still have some good bread. By the way, I'd love to cancel my classes tomorrow and start the weekend early, but I've got to keep pushing to get them ready for exams. So, sorry, I can't sleep at your place tonight."

"No, not tonight," he said. He sounded down.

I took my tea out to the car, turned the radio on loud and hit the road.

When I smelled the aroma of soup as I walked in the door of Pat's house, I knew how hungry I was. I cut up the bread while he filled two bowls, and we sat down to eat.

Though I was desperate for nutrition, I couldn't stop babbling about what I had been through. There's something about almost dying that makes you glad to be alive, ecstatic in fact.

I started by telling him how Tiffany pulled out a gun when I broke the news that her Picasso was a fake. By the time I was done telling him about how I talked her down and the police came, I had also told him who Detective Brian Murphy was, and why I had gone to see him about Lester Jappling two days earlier.

When I went to ladle a little more soup into my bowl, I remembered Pat still didn't know how John Ghent reacted to the story of Anne's forgery scheme. I felt a bit queasy while telling him Ghent was delighted to hear of his wife's treachery.

As I wiped my bowl clean with my last bite of bread, I mentioned that the deans had decided to suspend the normal rules of scholarship so they wouldn't alienate parents and donors.

Pat had long since finished eating. He looked exhausted. "Has it been only four days?" he asked.

"I know. It's hard to believe. I'm sorry I just blurted all that out, but I've been running from one thing to the next ever since we got back from New York, and each thing seemed more outrageous than the last. With all the driving to Shawville and back I never had the time or the energy to call you so we could get together for a meal and have a normal conversation."

"Not much has been normal for me either this week."

I took his hand. "How are you feeling?"

"Walking on eggshells."

"I can't imagine what it was like, growing up the way you did."

"The hard part is, it's not over."

I must have looked as confused as I felt.

"Dad's been gone seven years now," he said, "and I don't

feel any different. That's how trauma works, if it's bad enough and goes on long enough. It changes the brain. There's no way to change it back."

I didn't know whether to take this literally or to think it was an expression of his depressed thinking.

"Thanks for telling me about this," I said. "I'll do my best to learn more about it. I can learn how to recognize when it's happening and what to do. Maybe we could go together for counseling. I know you're a psychologist and you know all about it, but maybe a neutral third party could help us."

"Nicole . . ." He froze, unable to think what to say next.

"There is counseling for this, isn't there?"

"Yes, people go for counseling, and it helps, but there's only so much they can do. I can learn—I have learned—to make these episodes less frequent and less severe, but I will always be someone who can be triggered."

"But can you keep making them even less frequent and even less severe?"

"It's not that simple. Meditation is supposed to help, and I do some of that. Getting in touch with nature is supposed to help, which makes this campus perfect for me. Exercise helps, which is why I lift weights. I tried running, but it bothered my knees. But here's the catch: lifting weights has made me stronger, and that makes me more dangerous."

"Only if you're triggered," I said. "Most of the time you're just stronger. I can live with that."

"You don't know what you're saying."

"What do you mean? How bad can it be? It's not as if you're going to hurt me, is it?"

He looked at me, and looking into his green eyes was like staring into the depths of the ocean. "I could never hurt you," he said.

"Alright then, the rest I can live with."

He shook his head. "You don't want to live your life knowing that at any time I could do something like what I did on Sunday."

"Pat, as I told you, it wasn't that bad. Sure, you should probably avoid getting physical with people, but I was more scared when he put his hands on my shoulders."

"Think about it, Nicole. Jappling could still decide to take legal action. He could accuse me of assault. You could be called to testify as a witness. If we were married—I know we haven't seriously talked about marriage, but if we were—you could be bankrupted along with me if I had to pay damages."

I squeezed both his hands with mine. "And lightning could strike, or I could get cancer. Life is risky, and none of us gets out of it alive. There's no getting around that. But while we're here we have to have some fun, and I like having fun with you."

He had tears in his eyes.

I went on. "I'm not letting you go, Pat Gillespie. If you want to get rid of me, you'll have to come up with something better than PTSD."

He slid off his chair and knelt next to mine, which put us eye to eye. He wrapped his arms around me, and I hugged him back. I heard him sobbing and felt him struggle for breath.

When we'd both shed enough tears, he sat back on his heels. I used my napkin to wipe my face and his.

He smiled and said, "What a mess!"

"Yes. It is, and I love it. I love our mess." I kissed him. "Now I'm going back to my Rabbit Hutch and getting to bed before I fall asleep in your kitchen."

He stood up. "I'll walk you back. It'll do me good to stretch my legs and get some fresh air."

I gave him a skeptical look.

He smiled. "I know: We said no sleeping over tonight. I won't even come in. I'll just walk you to your door and say good night."

As we turned from Fellbach Circle onto College Avenue, I said, "I've decided we're going away somewhere this weekend. Let's talk tomorrow morning and figure it out. Someplace we've been before, so we don't have to think about it. We'll just eat take-out, and have picnics in parks, and take long walks. Someplace that has traffic and noise where we're not surrounded by trees."

"Sounds good."

Chapter 34

On Sunday evening, I dusted, swept, and generally tidied up my Rabbit Hutch while awaiting Abbie's arrival. She had texted that she was bringing lasagna from her favorite place in Pittsburgh and offered to share it. I told her to bring it to my place, since she had hosted our last meal.

After setting places at my cafe table, I got out the bottle of red wine I'd picked up when Pat and I were on our way back to campus earlier in the afternoon. We'd had a lovely couple of nights in Cincinnati. We weren't quite back to being our usual fun-loving selves, but we were feeling close to each other. Mission accomplished.

I read the front and back labels on the wine bottle, looking for some encouragement about its quality. After all, I had bought the "red table wine" that cost a dollar more. That's how one splurges on an assistant professor's salary.

I thought about opening it and seeing how it tasted, but decided not to. Although I'd seen Abbie's car go by half an hour ago, I didn't know how long it would be before she brought the lasagna over. If I tasted the wine, I knew I would keep sipping it, and I didn't want to use up my quota of wine before I started eating. Of course, if I poured only a single sip into the glass, and, after tasting it, rinsed my mouth out with water . . .

I was saved from this decision by a knock on my door. "It's unlocked," I yelled.

I heard, "Help!" from outside, and opened the door.

Abbie came in, using oven mitts to carry the covered pan.

"Prepare for Petretti's finest!"

"I remember it well. Pat and I went there with you and Sharon."

"That's right. You did."

Abbie dished up the plates while I poured the wine, and we sat down to eat.

"Just as good as I remember," I said.

"So, what's it been, two weeks?" Abbie asked.

"Seems longer."

"What have you been up to?"

"Do you remember I asked you about those two Picassos and whether they could be investments? Turns out they're both forgeries."

"Whoa! I'll bet that made a couple of millionaires very unhappy."

"It was a little more complicated than that. The man who asked me to look into it —the one whose wife was killed— thought it was hilarious. It turns out his wife knew she was buying a forgery and didn't pay much for it. He's decided to keep it as a memento of the kind of woman she was."

Abbie chuckled. "It takes all kinds, I guess. How about the owners of the other one? How did they take the news?"

"It wasn't news to Tiffany because Anne—the murdered woman—had already told her it was fake. That's why she killed Anne. Anne had set her up to buy it."

Abbie shivered. "Obviously I wasn't keeping up with local news while I was in Pittsburgh."

"I'm not sure how much of this has been in the news."

"So, how do you know what happened?"

"Tiffany told me right after I told her painting was fake."

"Wait! You told her it's fake, and she confessed to killing her friend?"

"Not right away. First, she pulled out the gun she used on Anne, pointed it at me, and fired off a few shots."

"What?"

"I managed to talk her down and get her to turn herself

in."

Abbie sat back and stared out the window for a moment. "In a way, I wish you hadn't told me this. Stop doing things that could get you killed!"

"Do you mean things like investigating the provenance of modern paintings?"

"You know what I mean."

We both took a minute to eat and drink some wine. The lasagna was just as heavenly as I remembered. The wine was okay.

Abbie smiled as she said, "You must be feeling pretty good about exposing art fraud and getting a murderer arrested."

"I'm not sure how I feel. I had a very strange day, last Tuesday."

"Strange how?"

"I drove over to Shawville to talk to the detective investigating the murder. This was before Tiffany confessed. I told him the sales manager at the gallery who sold Tiffany the forgery had a motive to kill Anne Ghent. Unfortunately, the detective wasn't interested."

"Why not?"

"He said since it was a shooting in a parking lot at night, the killer must be from 'a different class of people.' So, in his mind, a white guy, who definitely had a reason to kill her, was not a suspect, but a black guy, who had no connection to her other than being at the same mall at the same time, was a suspect."

"I can see how that would ruin your day."

"It wasn't just that. On the same day, I got an email from our dean, Vera Krupnik, telling me to grade a paper for my Modern Art class even though the student refused to acknowledge the source her paper was based on."

"Why would the student refuse?"

"I assume someone told her I was planning to accuse her of plagiarism if she admitted she used a source."

"Couldn't you tell her there was no question of plagiarism?"

"We never got that far. The dean told me to grade it as if there were nothing wrong with it."

"Why would she do that?"

"It turns out the student was the winner of a big scholarship in the School of Business, and therefore cannot be allowed to fail in any way."

Abbie shook her head as if trying to get rid of the thoughts inside.

I continued. "Tuesday was a day when nothing made sense. Motive is supposed to be important in a crime investigation, but the detective decided it wasn't. Acknowledging sources is necessary in scholarship, but the dean decided the student could skip it. Where does that leave me?"

Abbie blew air out between her lips. "I need more wine."

We picked up our glasses and moved to the canvas-sling beach chairs by my front window, which were only two steps away. Living in a Rabbit Hutch is so convenient.

Abbie swallowed some wine, cleared her throat, and said, "I don't know anything about the murder investigation, but I do know something about your academic problem. Do you remember, last year, there was talk of moving the Department of Economics from the School of Liberal Arts to the School of Business?"

"I heard something to that effect."

"I argued on the side of keeping my department in liberal arts because I didn't want to work in a business-school culture."

"Which means what?" I asked.

"A culture in which the ends justify the means. You win at all costs."

"Really? That may be true of some people in highly competitive businesses, but not university faculty. Our colleagues in business are scholars like we are."

Abbie smiled but looked sad. "There's a guy at Rutgers—in their School of Business, as a matter of fact—who has documented this with large-scale surveys. He asks students and faculty to define cheating and decide when they think it's acceptable to break the rules—things like that. It turns out people in business schools are much more, shall we say, flexible."

I'd never heard anything about this. "Why would that be?"

"Students go to business schools so they can get higher-paying jobs. Anything that doesn't help them do that they feel free to ignore. That same guy has broadened his surveys to all kinds of undergrad and graduate schools. The rule holds: In schools and departments that promise high-paying careers, students are more willing to cheat, and faculty are more willing to tolerate it."

It all made sense now. "Bayliss, the business-school dean, was in on this, the day I went to talk to Krupnik. So, it seems our dean just caved in to pressure from the School of Business."

Abbie nodded. "And, since the university has placed a multi-million-dollar bet on the business school, the pressure is huge."

"So, do we have to play by their rules now?"

"For the moment at least."

I took my last sip of wine and set my glass aside without pouring more. I needed to keep my head clear. "That's going to be a problem for me. I forced myself to grade that paper, but I don't know if I can go on doing things like that."

Abbie finished her wine. "I doubt you'll have to. You ran into the perfect storm: Your student was the poster girl for the biggest change ever to hit this school. I doubt that will happen again any time soon."

"I don't feel like waiting around to find out."

Abbie laughed. "We're back to the ever-popular topic of getting a job at a better school. Seen any good job listings, lately?"

"No, I haven't."

"It's not all bad here. You've got your own gallery where you can exhibit artists you like without having to worry about selling enough paintings to pay the bills."

"That's true. That's a good thing, but it's not enough."

"Apply for a sabbatical."

I started to laugh and almost choked. "I've only been here three years. I'll be due for one four years from now, but I don't think I can hold on that long."

"You don't have to. Our sabbatical policy is not based on years of service. The university provides for a certain number of research leaves every year. They go to whoever applies for them. Some years it's competitive, in which case a committee is formed to review the applications."

"How did the faculty negotiate that?"

"Actually, it was President Taylor's idea. I think he recognized we're a long way from research centers here. Offering research leaves to whoever has the best idea sent a signal that he didn't want the faculty to get complacent, teaching their same courses every year."

"Have you ever done this?"

"I had a semester off the year before you came here. I spent a week in New York and a couple of weeks in Chicago to use libraries and attend conferences, but mostly I stayed home with Sharon. I got a lot of writing done and published a couple of articles."

"Wow! I have to do this. When's the deadline?"

"They're all decided for next year, but start getting your application ready now and apply in the fall. At the end of fall semester, they'll name the recipients for the following academic year."

"I'm excited just thinking about this. But I wouldn't want to go away for the whole time. Pat's here, and I've gotten used to having my man around, if you know what I mean."

Abbie smiled. "For me, it's having my woman around,

but, yeah, I know what you mean. Get Pat to apply for the same semester. Maybe you can go away together."

A warm glow erupted in my belly and spread throughout my body. "I think this could work."

"You can make it work. Believe me, after living in a city for a semester and a summer, you'll start to think of this campus as your country home."

I got the wine bottle from the table, poured a glass for Abbie and half-a-glass for me. "Here's to making it work," I said.

We raised our glasses and drank.

Thank you for reading *Dark Picasso*.

If you enjoyed it, please help others find it by leaving a favorable review online.

Find more Nicole Tang Noonan Mysteries at:
www.RickHoman.com